I was born in Lowestoft in England, just up the coast from Southwold, and am lucky enough to have a holiday home in the town. It's a beautiful place with a quaint feel to it – very reminiscent of the Enid Blyton books that I enjoyed so much as a child. It's full of history and the east coast is blessed with all manner of interesting myths and legends, many of which find their way into the cases that the After-School Detective Club investigates. You'll find that many of the locations in this book are real, too, and even in their correct geographical positions. The lighthouse, for example, and the harbour are all as you would expect to find them, as is the old museum in Victoria Street. I can't promise that there are smugglers still operating on the sunrise coast, but they certainly were there in years gone by, and the tales of wreckers luring ships to their doom are lifted from the pages of local history.

I hope you enjoy your visit to the town, and that you'll come back again for another adventure with the team. We have lots more to share with you.

Mark Dawson
Southwold, 2021

The After-School Detective Club series:

The Case of the Smuggler's Curse

The Mystery of Ragnar's Gold
(available from June 2022)

THE AFTER
SCHOOL
DETECTIVE
CLUB

THE CASE OF THE SMUGGLER'S CURSE

Mark Dawson

WRITING WITH ALLAN BOROUGHS
ILLUSTRATED BY BEN MANTLE

WELBECK
FLAME

First published in 2022 by Welbeck Flame
An imprint of Welbeck Children's Limited,
part of Welbeck Publishing Group.
Based in London and Sydney.
www.welbeckpublishing.com

Text copyright © Unputdownable, 2022
Illustrations copyright © Ben Mantle, 2022

ISBN: 978 1 80130 006 3

Printed and bound by CPI Group (UK)

10 9 8 7 6 5 4 3 2 1

For Freya and Samuel

Lucy

Brave, loyal and athletic. She wants to be

an Olympian so don't get in her way . . .

Max

The geek with a wicked sense of humour.

Self-styled child genius – just don't tell his mum.

Joe

Adventurous, funny and a great cook – but
don't believe everything he says.

Charlie

Fierce as a lion, she loves her dog Sherlock more

than people. Don't ever call her Charlotte!

Sherlock

Loud bark, cold nose,

big heart – the fifth

member of the club.

1

THE FISHERMAN

Max Green stepped out onto the cold pavement and shivered in the icy night air. He waved goodnight to his after-school tutor, then slung his rucksack across his shoulders before setting off along the seafront. A frown creased his forehead as he felt the first spatters of rain. He hated coming home in the dark, especially in winter.

On the whole, Max liked living in the seaside town of Southwold. He particularly liked it in the summer, when the days were endless and there was nothing to do except to swim and lie on the beach. But winter in Southwold was a whole different ball game. The sea wind got right inside your duffel coat, the rain fogged your glasses, and there was nothing to do but stay indoors and wait for the warm weather. Southwold in winter was like the evil twin of Southwold in summer.

He walked along the deserted seafront with his head down against the wind, listening to the sound of the waves crashing on the beach and wishing he was at home with a cup of hot chocolate and slice of his mum's ginger cake. As he walked, a noise made him look up and peer into the darkness through his rain-spattered glasses.

A little way along the seafront, a group of older boys were hanging about on the street corner, laughing and pushing each other around playfully. Max recognised them immediately. It was Toby Watts and his mates. Max bit his lip. If he carried on walking, he would have to go right past them.

It'll be fine, he told himself. *Just look straight ahead and keep going, they probably won't even notice you.* Except it never really worked out that way, did it? He knew from bitter experience that Toby Watts and his goon squad *always* noticed him. There was something about Max that attracted their attention the way that blood in the water attracted sharks.

Max ducked behind a parked car and, when he was sure they were looking the other way, he scurried across the street to the wooden steps that led down to the beach. A year of encounters with Toby Watts had taught him that the best policy was usually to run away. If he walked along the beach, he would be able to sneak past them without being noticed.

But as Max descended the steps, he stopped in his tracks. There was someone standing by the shoreline, a hundred metres away. Max was used to seeing people walking their dogs on the beach at all hours but this man did not look anything like a dog walker. He was dressed from head to foot in heavy black oilskins, like a fisherman, and he stood with his back to Max, staring out to sea, his broad shoulders hunched against the wind.

Whether it was the way the man was standing so motionless, or the way he was completely ignoring the waves washing around his feet, there was something about him that made Max feel very uneasy.

He bit his lip and returned to the top of the steps. Toby Watts and his friends were still on the corner, laughing and hooting and having mock fights. Max weighed up his options. If he couldn't walk along the beach and he still couldn't get past Toby Watts, then there was only one thing for it. He would have to go home the long way.

Max turned and began to trudge miserably back along the seafront, heading in the opposite direction to his house. But he had not gone far when he stopped for a second time. Someone was sprinting towards him along the promenade from the direction of the pier: a girl, tall and dark-haired with a swinging ponytail. Her long legs pounded a regular rhythm on the pavement as she ran. Max smiled and breathed a sigh of relief. It was only Lucy.

Lucy Yeung and Max Green were about as different as it was possible for two people to be. Max was short, geeky and liked nothing better than spending an evening in his bedroom playing *Warlocks and Dragons* on his computer. Lucy on the other hand was tall, athletic and enjoyed being out of doors more than anything else. And yet, despite their differences, they had been the best of friends since their first day of school at St Enid's.

Lucy slowed down and broke into a broad grin as she approached. 'Hey, Max,' she called, glancing at his rucksack. 'Aren't you done with all the studying yet?'

'I don't know, Luce,' he called back. 'Aren't you done with all the running yet?' Max knew that Lucy's greatest ambition was to become an athlete and he scarcely ever saw her when she wasn't training hard for something.

She laughed in a good-natured way and fell into step beside him. 'What would you know about it?' she said. 'You've never done a day's exercise in your life.'

'This is true,' said Max. 'I keep telling you, exercise and me really don't mix.'

'And what on earth is this?' said Lucy. She leaned across him and hooked a finger under his tie, flipping it out of his jacket in a single movement. 'It looks like something my dad would wear.'

Max frowned as he smoothed his tie back into place. His fondness for ties was a never-ending source of amusement for Lucy. 'What can I say, Luce?' he said. 'I'm just a geek at heart. Besides, it's important to be well turned out. You never get a second chance to make a first impression.'

A puzzled look crossed Lucy's face. 'Aren't you walking in the wrong direction?' she said. 'Your house is back that way.'

'I thought I'd take the long way home,' he said breezily. 'Somebody told me I needed the exercise.'

He grinned but Lucy didn't laugh at the joke. She looked back at the boys gathered on the street corner, and Max wondered if she'd guessed that he was avoiding Toby Watts.

'By the way,' said Lucy, changing the subject. 'Thanks for helping me with my maths homework last week. I got an A. That's the best I've done all term.'

Max shrugged. 'My pleasure,' he said. 'Now if

you could just do PE for me, we'd be even.'

She smiled. 'I'm sure you'd enjoy exercise a lot more if you just did a little bit. How about a quick walk along the beach before we head home? Get some fresh air into those lungs of yours?'

At the mention of the beach, Max remembered the mysterious man he had seen earlier and felt a pang of nervousness. There had been something about the figure that had made him feel chilled inside, as if a sixth sense was warning him to keep away.

Max bit his lip. If he had been on his own he would never have dreamed of returning to the beach for fear of running into the ghostly figure again. But it was much easier to be brave when you had a friend like Lucy Yeung by your side.

Max grinned and looked up at his friend. 'Sure,' he said. 'A walk along the beach sounds great. What could possibly go wrong with that?'

2

NICE THINGS

Joe found his mother in her usual place, sitting at her dressing table and looking into the mirror. Penelope Carter continued applying her eye make-up with expert attention to detail, unaware she was being watched. When she caught sight of Joe hovering in the doorway, she flinched in surprise, smudging her mascara.

'Did you want something, Joe?' she asked, removing the smudge with a cotton bud.

'I was just wondering – have you heard from Dad yet?'

His mother sighed. Joe didn't know if she was annoyed by the smudge or by his question, but she was *definitely* annoyed. 'He's not coming home,' she said, starting to apply her make-up again. 'Not for a couple of weeks, anyway. This business trip is very important to him – he still has a lot to do.'

'A couple of weeks?' Joe couldn't keep the disappointment from his voice. 'But that means he won't be home for Christmas!'

Penelope Carter put down her make-up brush and turned towards him. 'I know you're disappointed, Joe,' she said. 'But you have to understand that the reason your father works so hard is so we can live in this lovely big house and you can have all those nice things in your bedroom. Would you rather not have those things, Joe?'

Joe pushed his hair back off his face and shrugged. 'Well... I suppose not...'

'There you are, then. You're eleven now, Joe. You should be able to deal with life's little disappointments.'

Joe hesitated. 'So, if Dad's not coming home, perhaps you and I could do something together on Saturday?'

Penelope Carter smiled, and it was like the sun coming out from behind a cloud. 'Of course we can,' she said. 'What would you like to do?'

Joe thought. 'Well, how about going to the beach?'

His mother frowned. 'I don't know, Joe,' she said. 'It's always so noisy down by the beach and the sun's not good for my skin.'

'Well, maybe we could take out the motorboat?'

She laughed lightly, and Joe thought how pretty her laugh sounded. 'The motorboat? Are you serious? You know how seasick I get. And besides, I'm having my hair done on Saturday morning and it will be ruined if I go out on that boat afterwards.'

Joe groaned. 'It's so unfair,' he complained. 'Whenever I want to do anything, Dad's always away and you're always busy. I mean, what is the point of living by the seaside if we don't take advantage of it?'

Penelope Carter gave a patient sigh. 'Don't be so dramatic,' she said. 'Your father and I can't drop everything each time you want to go to the beach.'

She smiled and cocked her head to one side, the way people did when you told them you'd missed your bus or when they heard that your goldfish had died. 'I know you're upset about Christmas, darling,' she said in a softer tone. 'But your father will be home very soon, and we'll do something special together then. Now be a good boy and run along; I have to be at the Benfleets' in less than half an hour.'

Joe sighed and trudged wearily back to his room. He knew he shouldn't have got his hopes up. His dad's job meant they were seldom together at Christmas, but it would have been nice, just for once.

He sat on his bed and looked around his room,

at the model planes hanging from the ceiling, the remote-controlled drone his dad had sent him for his birthday, and the expensive computer sitting on his desk. It was true, he did have nice things, but he would happily have given them all up if it meant they could be together.

There was a knock at the door, and his mother swished in, wearing her best coat. 'Now, I've left you something in the microwave, and there's some of those sausage rolls you like in the fridge. Do your homework, and don't go to bed late. I should be home by midnight.'

She reached out and lifted his chin with her gloved hand. 'Don't look so glum, darling,' she said. 'Why don't you invite a friend over for a couple of hours?'

Joe frowned and pulled his chin away. 'I haven't got any friends. Not since we moved here anyway.'

His mother gave him the dead-goldfish smile again. 'Give it time, Joe,' she said. 'You'll make new friends; I know you will. Now, I really have to dash. Remember what I said and don't go to bed late.' She bent down to air-kiss him so that she didn't smudge her make-up, then she swished out again, leaving only a cloud of expensive fragrance behind her.

As the front door slammed, Joe sighed and lay back on his bed. More than anything he didn't want to eat another microwave dinner on his own. What he really wanted to do was have some fun.

It had been nearly six months since they had moved to Southwold. It had been his dad's idea to live by the seaside and, at first, Joe had been excited. He imagined himself spending long days on the beach with his friends, learning to surf and cooking sausages on the barbecue. He imagined summer afternoons spent on the pier or exploring the coastline in the motorboat that his dad had said they were going to buy.

But the reality had been somewhat different. For a start, his dad's job meant that he was hardly ever at home and his mother seemed to hate everything about the seaside. Then he had discovered that most of the kids in his new school already knew each other very well and spent a lot of their free time going to each other's houses.

It was all very well having nice things, he thought, but it didn't mean much if you had no one to share them with.

Joe began to pace up and down his room. It was no good sitting here and feeling miserable, he told himself. If he was ever going to enjoy living by the seaside, he would have to find some friends from somewhere.

But there was no point in trying to meet anyone new in Southwold. He'd been trying to do that ever since they had moved here. If he was going to make friends, he would need to look further afield. And that meant he was going to have to pack a bag.

Moving quickly, he reached under the bed for his rucksack, then started to rummage in the wardrobe for the clothes he would need. Joe was determined to get some new friends, no matter how far he had to go to find them.

3

ON THE BEACH

Max and Lucy walked along the promenade with their heads down against the wind. Now that they had decided to go for a walk on the beach, Max was anxious to get off the street as quickly as possible to avoid being seen by Toby Watts but Lucy kept stopping to look up at the sky. 'Do you think it will be a white Christmas this year?'

'Of course not,' snorted Max. 'They only put snow on Christmas cards to get everyone in the holiday mood. It never snows at Christmas, at least not here. It just rains. Now *come on.*'

But Lucy had stopped again and was peering in the direction of the bus stop a short way up the road. Max followed her gaze and noticed a solitary figure sitting inside the shelter, a gangly boy with blonde hair plastered by the rain. He seemed to be crying.

'Do you think he's okay?' asked Lucy.

Max shrugged. 'I recognise him from school. He was one of the new kids this year.'

Lucy looked at the boy. 'Were we really that small once?'

'In case you hadn't noticed,' said Max drily, 'some of us are still that small.'

Lucy didn't reply and walked over to the boy. 'Are you okay?'

Joe Carter looked up in surprise at the very tall girl and the very short boy who were now standing in front of him. He had got completely soaked on his way to the bus stop and had then discovered that there were no more buses until morning. Realising that his plan to run away and make new friends seemed to be over before it had started, he had sat down and started to feel very sorry for himself.

Joe jumped up quickly, rubbing his eyes. 'I wasn't crying,' he said at once. 'It's just the rain, that's all.'

'If you say so,' said Lucy. She looked at the boy curiously. His clothes had expensive-looking labels, but they were completely unsuitable for the wet weather.

Max nodded towards the timetable on the bus-shelter wall. 'No more buses tonight,' he said.

'Oh.' Joe glanced around quickly. 'Yes, I know. I'm just waiting for... for some friends!' He brightened. 'Yes, some friends. They'll be along at any moment to pick me up, and then we're all going to a big party. I have lots of friends. I have so many friends I don't know what to do with them all.' He gave an unconvincing laugh.

'We'll take your word for it,' said Lucy. 'Well, if you're sure you're okay, we'll see you around.'

Max and Lucy turned away, but the boy started after them. 'Wait!' he said quickly. 'Perhaps I could come with you guys instead?'

'What about your friends?' asked Max.

The boy slung the rucksack over his shoulder and fell into step behind them. 'Don't worry, they won't mind. So, where are we going?'

Max and Lucy exchanged a glance. 'Nowhere special,' said Max. 'Just the beach. It's not as exciting as going to a party.'

'Oh, that's okay,' said the boy. 'I wasn't much in the mood for a party, anyway.'

Max rolled his eyes, and Lucy shrugged, but neither of them quite had the heart to tell the boy to go away. They descended the steps to the empty beach, feeling their feet sink into the soft, damp sand.

Instinctively, Max looked up and down the shoreline, but there was no sign of the mysterious stranger he had seen earlier and he allowed himself to relax. They turned left and passed beneath the old pier, walking away from the town. The great iron structure was now closed for the winter and looked like the skeleton of some vast sea monster that had washed up on the shore.

The rain had begun to ease a little, and Lucy took a lungful of the fresh, clean air. White-topped breakers sloshed around the iron girders of the pier and crashed on the sand in the darkness. Coming here reminded Lucy that the peaceful little town in which she lived was still on the edge of a wild and dangerous sea. It was the part of the beach she liked best of all.

'It's beautiful here, don't you think?' she said.

'I prefer it in the summer,' said Max.

'I know you two!' said Joe, still walking behind them. 'You're Lucy Yeung. You won the fifteen hundred metres in the interschool tournament last month.'

Lucy flashed him a quick smile.

'And you're Max Green. You're the school chess champion.'

'Three years running,' said Max. 'What did you say your name was?'

'Joe. Joe Carter.' He held out his hand.

Max looked at the hand for a moment and then gave it a quick shake. 'Charmed,' he said.

They left the pier behind and walked beside a row of colourful wooden beach huts, painted in brilliant shades of yellow, red and turquoise. 'The rain's finally stopped,' said Lucy. 'Shall we sit down for a bit?' She was resigned to the fact that this strange boy wasn't going away any time soon and, besides, she loved sitting on the beach at night and watching the waves.

Lucy approached one of the beach huts and brushed sand from the wooden steps before sitting down beneath the overhanging roof. Max sat beside her, and Joe sat on the other side, grinning at his two new-found friends.

'Hey,' he said, rummaging in his rucksack. 'Does anyone fancy a sausage roll? I brought some for the journey.' He pulled one from his bag and offered it to Max and Lucy. It looked battered and slightly damp, and they both shook their heads politely. Joe shrugged and took a bite, spilling pastry crumbs down the front of his shirt.

'What journey?' said Max after a while. 'I thought you said you were going to a party.'

For a moment Joe looked confused. 'Oh, that.' He laughed, spraying more crumbs. 'No, that wasn't really true.' He took another bite and then spoke with his mouth full. 'Actually, I was running away.'

'Running away?' Lucy's eyes widened. 'You mean like running away from home?'

'Sure,' said Joe. He crammed the last piece of sausage roll in his mouth and reached into the bag for another. 'I wanted to find some new friends. But hey.' He looked up and grinned. 'I don't need to do that now that I've found you two.'

Max and Lucy stared at the boy open-mouthed for a moment. Max was about to say that they weren't friends when they were interrupted by a loud barking coming from further down the beach.

'Now what?' grumbled Max. 'It's more crowded on this beach tonight than it is on a bank holiday.'

A small dog was running along the sand towards them, barking frantically. The dog had short legs and a barrel chest. He was mostly white with brown patches on his head and floppy ears. He scampered straight past Lucy and Max and came to a stop in front of Joe, still barking madly.

'He's got a big bark for such a small dog,' said Lucy.

'I think he likes me,' said Joe, evidently pleased to have made another friend.

'Don't flatter yourself,' said Max. 'I think he just likes sausage rolls.'

Joe broke off a piece of sausage and threw it to the dog, who caught it in mid-air, throwing back his head to wolf it down in a single gulp. No sooner had the dog swallowed the piece than he started barking again.

'Now you've done it,' said Lucy. 'You'll never get rid of him now.'

This news clearly delighted Joe, who began tearing off more pieces of sausage roll and throwing them to the dog. He roared with laughter each time the animal successfully caught a piece in his jaws. 'He's so scruffy-looking,' said Joe. 'I bet he doesn't have an owner. Perhaps I should take him home.'

No sooner had Joe spoken than there was a yell from along the beach. 'What do you idiots think you're doing?'

They turned to see a girl stalking out of the gloom towards them. She was short and very slight, with pale skin and brown hair tied in two long plaits. There was a pair of battered binoculars hanging around her neck.

Despite her small size, she wore an expression of complete fury. Her teeth were bared and her eyebrows were knitted together in a furious scowl. Her fists were clenched into bloodless knots, and she glared directly at Joe as she stomped up the beach.

'I think you just found his owner,' said Max. 'And she really doesn't look too pleased with you.'

4

WRECKERS

Lucy stared at the advancing girl. 'I've seen her around at school,' she murmured. 'I think her name's Charlotte Wells. She's always sitting in the playground by herself.'

'Yeah, that's because everyone's afraid of her,' said Joe in an urgent whisper. 'She's always going on about birds and wildlife and saving the planet and stuff like that, but she seems to hate people. Last month a boy in our class threw a stone at a seagull, and she got so angry that she punched him on the nose and made it bleed.'

As the girl drew closer, she started shouting again. 'Why are you feeding my dog?' she yelled.

'He's not yours. You've got no right. How dare you!'

Max stared at the girl in shock. He didn't think he had ever seen anyone look as angry as Charlotte Wells seemed to be right now. Her face was screwed up in a furious scowl, her fists were clenched tightly and her eyes flashed with fire. She looked like a small animal that was preparing to fight to the death.

Joe backed into the porch of the beach hut, with his hands held out in front of him defensively. 'I didn't mean anything,' he stammered. 'I just gave him a bit of sausage, that's all. He liked it. It's good for him.'

'Cheap sausage rolls are *not* good for him,' raged the girl. 'Or anyone else for that matter.'

'But they're not cheap,' protested Joe. 'My mum buys them special. They're organic. It says on the packet that—'

'I don't care what they are,' yelled the girl. '*I* take care of my dog, and no one else feeds him except for me. Got that?'

Joe was nodding frantically. 'S-sure,' he spluttered. 'Anything you say.'

'I'm sure Joe didn't mean any harm,' said Lucy. 'Did you, Joe?'

Joe shook his head vigorously, still trying to keep as far away from Charlotte Wells as possible.

'There you are,' said Lucy. 'So why don't you two make up and be friends?'

'Yeah,' said Max. 'Joe needs friends. And you both seem to get on so well together.'

Lucy shot Max a glare, and he shut up immediately.

Charlotte Wells folded her arms and clamped her mouth into a tight line. She narrowed her eyes at Lucy, and the older girl calmly returned her gaze. 'Alright, I'll let him off this time,' she said eventually. Then she jabbed an accusing finger at Joe, who flinched visibly. 'Just tell *him* not to come near my dog again.' She turned to her dog. 'Come on, Sherlock, it's time we were going.'

'Your name's Charlotte, isn't it?' asked Lucy as the girl turned to leave.

The girl glared at Lucy with fresh venom in her

eyes. 'No one ever calls me Charlotte,' she said through gritted teeth. 'My name's Charlie. C-H-A-R-L-I-E. Got that?'

'Alright, alright,' said Lucy. 'I was just trying to be friendly, that's all.'

'I don't need friends. Me and Sherlock do just fine together.'

'Yeah, you seem very well suited,' said Max. 'It looks like Sherlock's already picking a fight with someone else.' They all looked at the little dog, who seemed to have forgotten all about Joe's sausage rolls and was now barking angrily at something in the darkness.

'Is he always like that?' said Lucy.

'No,' said Charlie, looking puzzled. 'He's usually so well behaved. I don't know what's got into him. Hey, Sherlock, cut it out!' But it made no difference. The little dog kept barking as though his life depended on it.

'I think he's barking at someone over there,' said Joe, pointing. 'Up on those rocks, look.'

A hundred metres along the shoreline, the beach huts came to an end and the sea wall began: a concrete and stone barrier that protected the town from the worst of the winter storms. In front of the wall, hundreds of large granite blocks had been piled up in long lines that extended out into the sea.

Max wiped the rain from his glasses with his tie and then squinted into the darkness at the spot where Joe was pointing. Standing on top of the granite blocks at the farthest end of the sea wall was the same mysterious figure he had seen on the beach earlier. Max felt the same cold fear he had felt earlier, gripping his spine with icy fingers.

'What is that guy doing?' said Lucy. 'Doesn't he know it's really dangerous to stand up there on the sea wall? He could get washed away.'

'Do you think he's in trouble?' asked Joe. 'Maybe we should see if we can help?'

'Er... I'm not so sure that's a good idea,' said Max

in a weak voice.

'He's holding something,' said Charlie. She seemed to have forgotten her anger from a moment ago. She raised her binoculars and peered at the man. 'It looks like a lamp of some sort.'

As she spoke, a flame flickered, and a yellow glow bloomed in the darkness. 'It *is* a lamp,' said Lucy. 'Looks like he's signalling to someone.'

The figure had begun to wave his lantern back and forth so that it really did look like he was giving some kind of signal. But there didn't appear to be anyone else on the beach, apart from them, who could see it.

'Look,' said Charlie, pointing out to sea. 'There's a ship out there.'

Far out in the blackness, a faint light blinked on and off several times, as though it was answering the glow from the stranger's lamp. 'I know what he is,' said Joe, hopping up and down on the boards excitedly. 'He's a wrecker.'

Lucy gave him a blank look. 'What's a wrecker?'

'I read about them,' Joe explained. 'They used to stand on the shoreline and shine lights to lure boats onto the rocks so that they'd get wrecked. Then the wreckers would steal everything they could from the boat and leave the poor crew to drown.'

'A hundred years ago, maybe,' said Max. 'But I've never heard about there being any wreckers in modern times.'

'Well, he's certainly doing something odd,' said

Lucy. All the talk of wreckers had roused her curiosity, and the man did seem to be behaving very strangely. 'Perhaps we should take a closer look?'

'I'm not so sure,' said Max nervously. Now he saw the stranger again, all the fear he had first felt had returned. 'What if he turns out to be dangerous? I think we should stay here.'

'Sherlock!' yelled Charlie suddenly. 'Sherlock, come back here!'

The little dog had been barking continuously at

the stranger and had now decided that this was something he needed to investigate. Without waiting for permission, he bolted across the sand, heading straight for the strange man on the rocks.

'Sherlock!' cried Charlie again. There was a note of fear in her voice. 'Come back! You could get hurt.' She took off, sprinting across the sand after Sherlock.

Lucy stood up. 'Maybe we should go too,' she said quickly. 'They might need help.' Before Max could stop her, she had gone, racing after Charlie and her little dog.

'Wait for me!' cried Joe. He skipped down the steps and ran after Lucy.

Max watched them go with a horrified expression. 'Wait up, guys,' he shouted. 'I'm telling you this is a really bad idea.' Then he clambered wearily to his feet and began a slow, shuffling jog after them.

Lucy's long legs gave her the advantage, and she soon caught up with Charlie. They reached the sea wall at the same time, with Joe arriving a few moments later. Charlie grabbed Sherlock by the collar and held on to prevent him bolting again. By the time Max arrived, puffing and blowing, they were all standing in the shadows, peering at the stranger on the slippery rocks.

They could see the man quite clearly now. His black oilskins were slick with sea spray, and the rainhat, pulled low, made it impossible to see his face. He did not seem to have heard Sherlock's barking over the sound of the waves and was still looking out to sea. The light in his hand was an old-style lantern, which he swung steadily back and forth. Far out to sea they could see a distant answering light blinking on and off.

'What did I tell you?' said Joe. 'He's definitely a wrecker. You mark my words, there's going to be a shipwreck.'

'That's ridiculous,' said Lucy. 'But all the same, Sherlock really doesn't seem to like him. Maybe we should call the police.'

'And tell them what?' panted Max, still struggling to regain his breath. 'That they should arrest this guy just because some stupid dog thinks he's suspicious?'

'Sherlock is not a stupid dog!' Charlie flared at him. 'He's smarter than most humans.'

'Quiet!' snapped Lucy. 'We're supposed to be deciding what to do, not fighting amongst ourselves.'

'Oh no!' cried Joe. 'Look at Sherlock!'

While they had been arguing, Charlie had let go of Sherlock's collar, and the little dog had seized his chance. As soon as he was free, he leaped onto the granite boulders and made his way towards the stranger.

Sherlock scrambled over the rocks, scrabbling for purchase with his claws. He could smell that this man was up to no good. Humans never seemed to pay much attention to smells. They would walk around with their noses high in the air, missing all the interesting smells near the ground, and it never seemed to bother them. But Sherlock trusted his nose and this man smelled of trouble.

And, of course, that meant that he, Sherlock, would have to do something about it. After all, a man like that might hurt Charlie, and Sherlock could never allow such a thing to happen.

The children's yelling and Sherlock's barking cut across the noise of the waves, and the man turned and noticed them all for the first time. He lowered the lamp and glared at them, clearly not happy to find that he was being observed.

But when he saw Sherlock bearing down on him, he snarled. His face was still partially hidden in the shadows, but his mouth was now visible, lips pulled back to expose a mouthful of crooked teeth. He bent down and picked up a rock, raising it high above his head before hurling it at Sherlock. The rock missed the little dog by a whisker, sailing over his head before bouncing into the sea. The man roared in frustration; it was a sound filled with so much anger and hatred that it chilled their blood.

The roar did not stop Sherlock, though. The little dog was now more determined than ever to protect Charlie. As the man bent down to pick up a second rock, Sherlock leaped and caught the leg of the man's trousers in his teeth.

The man yelled at the little dog and there was a fierce tussle as he tried to free himself. Sherlock held on with grim determination, worrying at the man's trouser leg until the material came suddenly free with a loud ripping noise. Sherlock was caught by surprise. With the piece of material still clamped in his mouth, he tumbled backwards over the slippery rocks and plunged into the oily waters below.

Charlie screamed again. 'Sherlock!' she cried. She turned to the others. 'He's fallen into the water. He'll be killed by the rocks. Please, somebody help him!'

5

SHERLOCK IN TROUBLE

For a moment nobody moved. Max and Joe stared in shock as Charlie screamed for her dog. Then Lucy sprang into action, jumping down onto the sand next to Charlie.

The waves were crashing heavily against the granite rocks, and a fierce undertow had already pulled the little dog several metres offshore. Sherlock was trying valiantly to swim against the current, but each time he came a little closer to the beach, the waves would drag him back out again. Lucy could see that he was beginning to tire.

'He'll be drowned!' cried Charlie. 'I have to do something.' She tore off her hoody and began to wade out towards Sherlock. Almost immediately a large wave knocked her over. It was only Lucy's quick action in grabbing hold of her arm that stopped Charlie from being dragged out too.

'You can't go out there, Charlie,' she cried, gripping her arm tightly. 'The waves are too strong.'

Charlie struggled to break Lucy's grip, but the older girl held on fast. They could see that Sherlock was getting weaker now and visibly struggling to keep his head above the water.

'Somebody throw him a rope!' cried Joe.

'We haven't got a rope, stupid!' yelled Lucy.

'We could form a human chain,' shouted Max above the roar of the waves. 'If we link up, one of us might be able to reach him and pull him back in.'

'He's right,' shouted Lucy. 'Quick, everyone, join hands.'

They lined up on the shingle and grasped each

other's wrists. Charlie wanted to go at the front so she could reach Sherlock herself, but Lucy wouldn't let her. 'It's too deep,' she told Charlie. 'And you're not as tall as me. Let me go first.'

Even in her panicked state, Charlie saw the sense of what was being said and agreed. Holding on to Charlie's wrist, Lucy began to wade into the black sea. She gasped for breath as the icy waters soaked through her thin tracksuit.

Charlie followed Lucy into the water and reached behind for Joe's hand as he waded in after her. Last of all came Max, the shortest. He clutched Joe's wrist with both hands, gritting his teeth and digging his heels into the shingle to stop them all being pulled out to sea.

Edging her way out, Lucy began to wade forward, still clutching Charlie's wrist. She could feel the undertow pulling against her legs and threatening to drag her into the deep water. The sea was up to her chest now, and she felt dizzy from the cold, but she was only a metre or so

from Sherlock. The little dog was nearly exhausted, he was struggling to keep his head above water and she could hear his pathetic whimpering as the waves washed over him.

Lucy stretched out her arm as far as she could, pulling against the others so that even Max was up to his waist in water. But Sherlock was still just out of reach.

Then a huge wave surged forward, pushing the little dog towards her just enough for Lucy's fingers to hook beneath his collar. She dragged him closer as the big wave crashed down, washing them back towards the beach and drenching them all in freezing water.

There were several seconds of coughing and spluttering as they disentangled themselves from the sodden heap. Then, with a desperate cry, Charlie fell on Sherlock, pulling him close and covering him with kisses.

'Oh, Sherlock,' she sobbed. 'I'm so sorry. It's all my fault. I should have held on to you more tightly. I'm so sorry. I'm so sorry.'

Sherlock himself looked shaken and a little wobbly. There was a small cut on his hindquarters, but otherwise he seemed unharmed. He whined a little and licked Charlie's face as she hugged him close, but very soon his tail began to wag again.

'Well,' said Max as he watched the happy reunion, 'I didn't expect to be doing *that* tonight.' Then he remembered something, and his face fell. 'Oh no! I forgot to take off my rucksack. My books will be ruined.'

'I'm just glad Sherlock's okay,' Lucy said. 'For one terrible minute I thought we'd lost him.'

Still clutching her dog, Charlie turned to the others. She looked pale and sick from the shock. 'Thank you,' she said weakly. 'Thank you for saving Sherlock. He means the world to me. I don't know what I would have done if... if...'

'It's okay,' said Lucy quickly. 'I'm glad we could help. He certainly is a brave little chap, tackling that guy all by himself.'

'The wrecker!' cried Joe, looking around. 'He's gone.'

It was true. In the excitement of rescuing Sherlock, the mysterious stranger had disappeared. What was more, there was no sign of the twinkling light out at sea either.

'I guess that means there won't be any shipwrecks tonight,' said Joe. 'Chalk one up to the good guys.'

At that moment it began to rain, stinging their faces and reminding them of just how cold they all were.

'I'm freezing,' said Max suddenly. His teeth were chattering so hard that he could barely get the words out.

'Me too,' said Lucy. She got up and slapped her arms vigorously, trying to warm herself, but it was of little use. The bitter sea and the heavy rain had driven the cold deep into their bones, and they were all shivering violently now.

'We have to get warm,' she said. 'And quickly,

or we could develop hypothermia out here.'

'Get warm how?' said Max. 'We can't exactly rub two sticks together, can we?'

Charlie stood and picked Sherlock up in her arms. 'I'll have to take him home,' she said. 'He's shivering, and he'll get a chill if I don't get him dry soon.'

'It's a long way back to town,' said Lucy, looking along the beach. 'We'll all be frozen solid by the time we get there.'

'I know a place we can go,' said Joe suddenly. 'It's perfect. And it's really close by.'

Max grunted. 'This isn't some made-up place, is it? Like those imaginary friends of yours?'

'No, honestly,' said Joe. 'I can take you there now.'

Lucy frowned at Joe. 'This had better be true, Joe,' she said. 'I'm serious. We need to get warm quickly.'

'Well, come on then,' said Joe. 'There's no time to lose.'

Before any of them could ask another question, Joe jumped to his feet and started back down the beach in a stiff-limbed trot. 'Hurry up,' he yelled back over his shoulder. 'Stop dawdling, you lot.'

Lucy shrugged. 'Well, I suppose we'd better follow him,' she said. 'At least it's in the right direction.'

Charlie scowled. 'If he's lying about this, I'm going to kill him with my bare hands.'

'If he's lying,' said Max, 'I'll hold him down while you do it.'

6

THE BEST PLACE IN THE WORLD

Joe led them back in the direction of the town. Nobody spoke as they struggled across the damp sand in a long line. The sea wind cut through their wet clothes, making them feel stiff and slow. Lucy was worried. She knew how dangerous it could be if they were exposed to the cold and wet for too long.

As though reading her thoughts, Charlie called out from the back of the group, 'How much further? I'm worried about Sherlock. He's shivering like anything.'

'Don't worry, we're here,' said Joe. He brought

them to a halt at a row of beach huts.

The last beach hut in the line was painted in summer sea colours of blue and turquoise. It had two wooden steps and white wooden handrails. Joe crouched, reached beneath a plank, and retrieved something from underneath. It was a key.

'Got it!' he said triumphantly. 'I just hope the lock hasn't rusted up.'

The others stared in amazement at the beautiful little beach hut. 'Is this really yours?' said Lucy.

'Yeah.' Joe nodded. 'My dad bought it when he was trying to persuade my mum that we should move to Southwold.'

'He *bought* it?' said Max. 'I asked my mum and dad if we could hire a beach hut for a day last summer, but they said they cost far too much money.'

Joe shrugged. 'I don't know how much Dad paid for it, but I remember him telling his friends that he'd "paid an arm and a leg for a glorified shed".'

Lucy ran a hand along the white-painted rails. 'Well, I think it's beautiful,' she said. 'Your family must spend all their time here when the weather's nice.'

Joe made a face and looked down at his shoes. 'We only came the once,' he said. 'Mum hated it. She said the sand got everywhere, and it wasn't "exclusive" enough. I don't really know what that means, but I remember they had a big row about it, and we had to leave early. After that, Dad locked it up and said he was going to sell it the next day. But then he went away on business, and I think he forgot all about it.'

Max and Lucy stared at Joe. Neither of them could imagine their families owning something as wonderful as their own beach hut, let alone forgetting all about it.

Their thoughts were interrupted by Charlie. 'If you're all done admiring the beach hut,' she said, 'I need to get Sherlock inside. Now!'

Joe jiggled the key in the lock. It was crusted

with salt and took him some time to work it free, but suddenly the door swung open. Joe disappeared inside, and the others squeezed through the entrance after him. Joe scrabbled around in the dark until he found a box of matches and lit a small lamp standing in the corner.

A warm yellow glow filled the little cabin, illuminating a tidy space with faded blue rugs laid on the wooden floor. There was a low counter along one wall and wide bench seats with colourful throws and fat squashy cushions.

'Oh my!' said Lucy. 'I never saw a beach hut as lovely as this one before.'

'You could live in here,' said Max.

Joe struck another match and crouched down beside the heater. There was a low *whoomph*, and a yellow flame sprang up. The children gathered around it with outstretched hands, sighing with pleasure as the warm glow seeped into their fingers.

'There are towels in here,' said Joe, opening a cupboard. 'And some bathrobes too. Mum sent off for them from a shop in London, but we never used them.'

Charlie immediately grabbed a thick towel and sat down in front of the fire to dry Sherlock. The little dog shivered as she worked, rubbing him vigorously to get some warmth back into his muscles.

Max grabbed another towel and wrapped it around himself. The towel was dry and fluffy and covered him down to his feet. Gratefully he peeled off his wet socks and jeans and spread them out on the floor near to the fire. Then he took off his tie and draped it carefully over a chair, smoothing out the damp wrinkles as he did so.

Lucy had wrapped herself in a bathrobe and was wringing out her wet tracksuit at the door. 'This is the best place in the world,' she said.

Joe beamed and puffed out his chest as his new friends made themselves comfortable. 'Er, how about a drink?' he said. 'I can fix us something hot.' There was a camping stove on the counter with a shiny new kettle on top. Joe reached up and took down some tins from a shelf, prising off the lids to inspect their contents. 'There's some hot chocolate in here,' he said. 'And bottled water that I can boil in the kettle.'

'Hot chocolate would be the best thing ever right now,' said Max. Still wrapped in his towel, he had installed himself in a corner of the hut and was making himself comfortable amongst the cushions. 'I don't suppose you've got anything to eat in there, have you?'

Joe opened another cupboard and poked around inside. 'There's some shortbread biscuits in here,' he said. 'They haven't been opened, so they should still be alright.'

At the mention of biscuits, Sherlock gave a loud bark and jumped up from Charlie's lap, with his tail wagging and his eyes fixed on the packet. Next to sausages, biscuits were absolutely Sherlock's favourite thing.

The children laughed at the sudden interruption. 'Well, he seems to be back to his old self,' said Lucy. She noticed Charlie's anxious expression and laid a hand on her shoulder. 'Don't worry,' she said. 'I'm sure he'll be absolutely fine.'

'And I'm sure he'd like one of these,' said Joe,

taking a biscuit from the packet. Then he paused and glanced nervously at Charlie. 'If... you'd like to give him one, that is.' He held out the packet towards her.

Charlie looked at the packet and then at Joe. 'It's okay,' she said. 'You can feed him a biscuit if you want to.'

Joe beamed and bent down to offer the biscuit to Sherlock, who took it gently from Joe's hand, then ate it noisily on the rug. At that moment the kettle warbled to life, and, in no time, Joe was handing around steaming mugs of hot chocolate and shortbread. The biscuits were a little soggy, and the hot chocolate was quite lumpy, but the children agreed that they were the best things they'd had to eat and drink all year.

'I could happily sleep in here,' said Max from his corner. 'It's more comfortable than my bed. Toby Watts would never find me in here.'

'If my family had a place as nice as this,' said Lucy, snuggling down in the opposite corner,

'I think I'd come here every day. If my dad would let me have the time off from training, that is,' she added.

'I came here by myself once or twice,' said Joe. 'But it's not much fun if you don't have friends to share it with.'

'So, what about you, Charlie?' said Lucy, noticing that the girl had become very quiet. 'Wouldn't you like a place like this to hang out?'

Charlie shrugged. 'It's okay, I guess,' she said without looking at Lucy. 'But most of the time, me and Sherlock are just out on our own.' She held up her binoculars. 'We go bird spotting in the dunes, so a place like this would be wasted on the two of us. I think we can manage fine without it.'

Lucy frowned. She found the fierce little girl very strange indeed and would have liked to know more about her, but Charlie clearly wasn't the talking kind.

But if Charlie was quiet, then Sherlock was the opposite. The little dog was having the time of his life. He ate three more biscuits, including one he managed to sneak out of the packet when no one was looking. Then he barked and rolled over and allowed his tummy to be tickled as the children took turns petting him.

Sherlock was very glad that Charlie had decided to be friends with these children, particularly the tall girl who had pulled him out of the water. They were definitely good people, he decided as he curled up for a sleep in front of the fire.

Satisfied that his guests were well provided for, Joe settled himself on the couch between Lucy and Max with his cocoa. 'So,' he began, 'what are we going to do about our ghostly wrecker?'

Max snorted scornfully. 'There's no such thing as ghosts,' he said. 'Or wreckers either for that matter.' Now that he was safe and warm in the beach hut, the thought of the mysterious stranger did not seem nearly as scary.

'Well, whoever he was,' said Lucy, 'he was behaving very suspiciously. Maybe we should tell the police what we saw?'

'We don't have any evidence,' said Joe. 'The police would probably just tell us off for mucking around on the sea wall.'

'Besides,' said Max, 'he didn't actually do anything except stand around with a light in his hand. There's no crime against that.'

'He *did* hurt Sherlock,' said Charlie, her grey eyes flashing. 'And I'll never forgive him for that. Sherlock could have been...' She paused. 'He could have...' She stopped speaking altogether and bit her lip as though the next words were too awful to say.

Hearing his name mentioned, Sherlock was suddenly awake. He jumped up and licked Charlie's face. The girl was taken by surprise, and the change in her expression was instantaneous. She laughed. 'Cut it out, Sherlock. Your tongue's all covered in biscuit crumbs.'

The others laughed too, and pretty soon Sherlock was jumping up on the cushions again and taking it in turns to lick their faces so that it made them all giggle. 'Thank you,' said Charlie suddenly. 'Thank you all for helping me to save Sherlock. I don't know what I would have done if you hadn't been there.'

Max and Joe looked bashful and shrugged as though wading into the sea in the middle of winter had been nothing at all. Lucy smiled. 'You're welcome,' she said.

'And I'm sorry I was so horrible to you earlier,' said Charlie to Joe. 'It's just that Sherlock and me are on our own so much that we've never really trusted anyone else before.'

Joe went pink and pushed his floppy hair out of his eyes. 'That's okay,' he said. 'I wish my mum would let me have a dog, but she says they jump all over the furniture. I think Sherlock's the best dog in the world.'

Charlie beamed when Joe said this, and it was like the sun coming out from behind a cloud. 'Yes, he is!' she said. 'And you're welcome to feed him or pet him any time you want to. All of you are.'

She stood up and placed her mug on the counter. 'Thanks for the hot chocolate. But me and Sherlock have to go. It's getting late.'

'Oh no, is that the time?' Max had pulled his phone from the waterproof pouch inside his rucksack and was staring at it in horror. 'My folks will be furious. I still have homework to do.'

Joe laughed. 'I never usually bother with my homework, and Mum never asks.'

'My mum *always* asks,' said Max as he retrieved his tie. 'And she regards not doing your homework as a hanging offence.'

Lucy looked at her fitness watch and made a face. 'I've got to get back too,' she said. 'My dad thinks I'm still out running.'

A look of dismay crossed Joe's face. 'Wait, don't all go just yet,' he said. 'We were just getting to know each other. Stick around. I'll make some more hot chocolate.'

But the others were already on their feet, pulling on damp jeans and socks and collecting their things. Joe's party seemed to be over.

'At least let's agree to meet up again,' he said. 'We could try to find out some more information about the wrecker.'

'And how exactly are we going to do that?' said Max, stuffing a pulpy exercise book back into his bag.

'There's a museum in town,' said Joe. 'I had to go there when we did a school project on the lighthouse. They might be able to tell us something about wreckers. Come on, it'll be fun to hang out together. Shall we say tomorrow at ten o'clock?' He looked at each of them eagerly.

Charlie looked uncertain. 'I don't know,' she said. 'Me and Sherlock are pretty busy tomorrow.'

Max shrugged. 'I can't promise anything, either,' he said. 'Saturday morning is usually when I help out in the shop. But if I don't see you, good luck with catching the wrecker.' He stood in the open doorway. 'Coming, Luce?'

Lucy felt pained by the look on Joe's face, and

she gave him a sympathetic smile. 'I can't promise anything either,' she said. 'But we will try. Thanks again for the hot chocolate.' She paused and looked around the cabin. 'This really is the best place in the world.'

7

CAPTAIN TOM

Next morning Joe hurried through the High Street on his way to the museum, feeling anxious. What if they didn't come? What if his new friends decided to stay home or go for a walk on their own with the dog? After the fun he'd had the previous night, he didn't think he could bear to spend the day all by himself.

His mother had arrived home late, and she was still in bed when he let himself out of the house and headed down the hill towards town. The day was fresh and bright after the miserable weather of the night before. Joe jogged past shopkeepers laying out fruit and veg or placing freshly baked loaves in their shop windows. He didn't stop to speak to anyone or even pause to glance up at the towering, whitewashed walls of the lighthouse in the centre of town. He didn't stop running until he reached the squat little museum at the end of Victoria Street, with its curly-topped roof that reminded him of the gingerbread house from the fairy tales.

The clock on St Edmund's Church read ten minutes to ten. He waited patiently, watching the Saturday morning shoppers heading into town, and looking up and down the street for any sign of his friends. But by the time the clock struck quarter past the hour, his face was gloomy. They weren't coming.

With a heavy heart he turned away from the museum and had just started the long walk home when there was a shout from behind him. 'Hey, Joe. Wait up.'

He turned to see Lucy pounding along the pavement towards him in a yellow tracksuit.

'Hi!' he called back. 'You actually came!'

'Don't sound so surprised,' she said, coming to a halt beside him. 'Sorry I'm a bit late. Dad was furious that I was out so long last night. I had to wait until he went to work before I could get out again.' She looked around. 'Where are the others?'

Joe shrugged. 'Couldn't make it, I guess,' he said. 'But I'm glad you're here, at least. Shall we go in?'

They turned towards the museum entrance and were about to go inside when another shout echoed down the street. 'Hey! Wait for me!'

They turned to see the extraordinary sight of Max riding on a sleek-looking skateboard. The board glided noiselessly along the street towards them without any apparent effort on Max's part, coming to a smooth stop right outside the museum.

'What *is* that thing?' said Lucy.

'Battery-operated skateboard,' said Max. 'I made it myself out of spare parts from the shop.'

Lucy smiled. She knew that Max's parents ran a computer shop and that Max was extremely clever at making all kinds of gadgets in his bedroom. The skateboard was a first, though.

Joe looked at it enviously. 'That's the coolest thing I ever saw.'

'Thanks,' said Max, picking up the machine and stowing it under his arm. 'Believe me, this is how everyone will travel in the future. So, have you found out anything about your "ghost wrecker" yet?'

'We were just about to go in,' said Lucy.

Joe took one last look along the street. 'I was hoping Charlie and Sherlock might come too,' he said. 'But I guess they went bird spotting instead.'

The trio entered the front door and stood for a moment, eyes wide with amazement. The museum was tiny but crammed full of glass cases, prints, photographs, and strange contraptions from bygone days. A crusty-looking gentleman with white whiskers and a naval cap gave them a nod from his chair in the corner, then went back to his newspaper.

They began to explore the contents of the museum, calling out to each other with delight when they found something new. A glass case along one wall was filled with bones, fossils and even mammoths' teeth that had been dug up locally. Others held moths, butterflies, stuffed birds and a scale model of a wooden sailing ship, complete with cloth sails.

There was a pair of giant wooden oars hanging on the walls that were said to belong to a Viking longship, and cannonballs that had actually been fired in a sea battle. Joe was fascinated by a display of guns and swords, and Lucy liked looking at the old children's toys fashioned out of painted wood and tin. Max was particularly taken with the medicine chest that had a special compartment for poisons.

But, however hard they looked, they could find no mention of wreckers or ghosts or anything that might explain the mysterious stranger they had seen the night before.

'I've had enough of this,' said Max after an hour of looking. 'There's nothing that can help us in here, and I need some sunlight. It's so dark and musty in this place.'

With heavy hearts they filed out of the museum and back onto the pavement, blinking in the winter sunlight. Standing outside, they found a familiar small figure with plaited hair and a small dog sitting by her side.

Sherlock barked with delight at seeing the other children again. He jumped up and licked their hands and scampered around their feet until Charlie scolded him, and he sat down with a shame-faced expression.

Joe laughed. 'Charlie!' he said. 'I knew you'd come.'

Charlie shrugged. 'I didn't think they'd let Sherlock in the museum, so we waited until you were finished. So how did you all get on?'

'We didn't find very much,' said Joe. 'I mean, there's loads of interesting stuff in there. But we couldn't find anything about ghosts.'

'So, it's ghosts you're looking for, is it, young man?' said a voice from behind them.

They turned to see the crusty old gentleman they had seen inside the museum. He wore a thick navy pea-jacket, buttoned up to the top, and a blue and white spotted scarf around his neck and he carried a cane. His naval cap was pushed back on his head, and he was watching them with sparkling blue eyes. He looked like something that had stepped out of a book about ancient seafarers.

Joe blinked. 'Er, y-yes,' he stammered. 'We were looking for information about local ghosts.'

'It's for a school project,' added Lucy quickly.

'Not that we believe in ghosts ourselves, you understand,' said Max.

The old man nodded sagely. 'Aye, there's plenty around here that don't believe in ghosts,' he said. 'All I know is...' He leaned towards them and lowered his voice to a dramatic whisper. 'It makes little difference to the ghosts whether you believe in them or not.'

The children stared at him. Lucy was the first to speak. 'Didn't we see you inside the museum?'

The old man nodded. 'That you did,' he said. 'Thomas Crofford's the name, though round here most people call me Captain Tom.' He pointed to where the lantern panes of the lighthouse were visible at the end of the street above the other buildings. 'I was the lighthouse keeper there for thirty years. But nowadays I just help out in the museum when I can. There's not much I don't know about Southwold's ghostly past. Not that you believe in that sort of thing, of course,' he added with a wink at Max.

'I believe in them,' said Joe quickly. 'So, are you saying that there really are actual ghosts, right here in Southwold?'

'Bless my soul, I reckon there's more ghosts than there are people in these old buildings,' he said with a laugh. 'I tell you what, I've just stepped out for a sit-down on those benches.' He nodded towards the churchyard across the street. 'If you've got a minute or two to spare, I'll see if I can help you out with your school project.'

Without waiting for an answer, Captain Tom strode across the street towards a bench that overlooked the gravestones in the churchyard. The children looked at one another and then followed. Max noted that Captain Tom walked with a strange rolling gait, like a man who has spent a lifetime walking on an unsteady ship's deck.

The old man settled on the bench as the children gathered around him. He rested his hands on his cane and surveyed them carefully. 'Very well,' he said. 'So, what is it you'd like to know about the ghosts in this town?'

They looked at each other nervously. Joe licked his lips. Up until now he had been certain that the strange figure they had seen on the beach had been a wrecker or a ghost, or both. But speaking about it in front of an adult made him feel foolish.

'We... heard a story,' he said slowly. 'Someone we know told us they saw a man carrying a lamp down by the sea wall. They said he was signalling to a boat out at sea. We... I mean *they* thought he might be a wrecker.'

'Or a ghost,' added Max.

'Or the ghost of a wrecker,' said Joe.

Captain Tom's brow furrowed. 'Well,' he said after a long wait, 'I've not heard many stories about wreckers in these parts. Wrong sort of coastline around here, see. But I've heard a lot of ghost stories in my time, and I reckon your friends might have seen the Spectre of Southwold Sands.'

'A spectre!' gasped Max.

'Here in Southwold?' gasped Joe.

'Is that a real thing?' said Lucy.

Captain Tom shrugged. 'Real enough to those who've seen him,' he said. 'They say he's the departed soul of a fisherman who lived in these parts two hundred years ago. Legend has it that one night he was lost at sea in a dreadful storm and feared he would surely drown. He was so afraid that he prayed to the spirits of the sea to deliver him home safe. It just so happened that, at that very moment, a mermaid was passing by and heard his prayer. She appeared from the waves beside his boat and offered to guide the fisherman to safety, but only if he would marry her and make her into a human bride.'

'A mermaid?' said Lucy, her eyes wide. 'So, what did he do?'

'What could he do?' said the old man. 'The fisherman agreed to the deal, and he let the mermaid take him back to the harbour and to safety. But fear is a strange thing. The moment a man feels safe again, he forgets all about it. As soon as he was safely back on dry land, he laughed at the mermaid and told her he wouldn't marry her because he was due to be wed to his childhood sweetheart. The mermaid was furious. She cursed him and swore that if he or any of his loved ones ever went to sea again, she would claim them for her own.'

'Somehow, I'm guessing this didn't end well,' said Max.

Captain Tom's eyebrows knitted together in a thick white hedge. 'It did not,' he said gravely. 'The fisherman was worried enough about the mermaid's curse that he gave up fishing altogether, and he forbade any of his family from ever going to sea.'

There was a pause. 'A year passed, and the fisherman forgot all about the mermaid as he made preparations to marry his sweetheart. But, on the day of their wedding, his bride-to-be decided to surprise her husband by catching a fresh crab for their wedding supper. She went down to the boatyard and took out his old fishing boat, forgetting all about her promise to stay away from the sea.'

The children were hanging on the captain's every word. 'What happened to her?' asked Joe in a whisper.

'As soon as she was out at sea, a terrible storm blew in from the north. The storm was so fierce, it was like something from hell itself. It smashed the little boat and drowned the poor girl in an instant. When the fisherman found out what had happened, he knew it was the work of the mermaid, and that he was to blame for the death of his bride. The poor man was so distraught that he threw himself into the sea and was drowned too. The mermaid's revenge was complete.'

'That's terrible,' said Lucy.

Captain Tom nodded. 'Terrible it might have been,' he said. 'But he should have known better than to cross a sea spirit. They say it's his ghost that still walks the sands, with a lantern in his hand, looking for his lost bride. They also say that it's an ill omen for anyone who sees him.'

'An "ill omen"?' asked Joe. 'What's one of those?'

'It means that something bad is going to happen,' said Captain Tom in a dark voice.

'You don't really believe those old tales, do you?' asked Charlie. 'All that stuff about mermaids and curses and ghosts. It's not real.'

'An old tale it might be,' said Captain Tom, 'but there's plenty around here that take it seriously enough.' He stood up and slipped his pipe back into his pocket. 'Now, if you'll all excuse me, I need to be getting back to my duties. But if I were you,' he added, 'I'd warn your friends to stay away from the sea wall on a winter's night. After all, you never know when you might see the Spectre.'

8

THE HARBOUR MASTER

Nobody spoke as they watched the old man disappear back inside the museum. Then Joe shivered. 'Brr, that tale's given me the creeps. Do you believe all that stuff about the mermaid's curse? Is something really bad going to happen to us just because we saw the fisherman?'

'You idiot,' snapped Charlie. 'He was just pulling your leg. There's no curse, and there's no ghostly fisherman either. He was just trying to frighten us to make us stay off the sea wall.'

'Still, it was a pretty good story,' said Max. He felt suddenly chilly and rubbed his arms to keep warm.

Even though he was not sure he believed in ghosts, he had to admit that the old man's tale had made the hairs on the back of his neck stand up.

'Well, after all that spookiness, I think we need something to take our minds off things,' said Lucy. 'How about we all go for an ice cream? My treat.'

'An ice cream!' said Max. 'Are you nuts? It's the middle of winter.'

'So what?' asked Lucy, grinning. 'I love ice cream at any time of year. I hardly ever get to eat sweets with all my training, but I'll always make an exception for ice cream.'

'Nowhere sells ice cream at this time of year,' said Joe.

'Not true,' said Lucy. 'There's a kiosk at the end of the harbour where they sell ice creams all year round. It's where I go for my secret supplies.'

'The harbour's miles away,' complained Max.

'It's less than a mile along the sand dunes,' said Charlie. 'Me and Sherlock walk it a lot. And besides, I like ice cream too.' She caught Lucy's eye and gave her the smallest of smiles.

At the mention of the word 'walk', Sherlock raised his head and barked agreement. On Saturday mornings, he and Charlie always went for long walks, and he could not understand why they had spent so long in one place today. Museums were definitely not the sort of thing that interested dogs.

'That settles it, then,' said Lucy. 'Come on, Max. The walk will do you good.'

They ignored Max's groans of protest and headed off through the town, with Sherlock leading the way, hoovering the pavement for smells as they went. They cut through an alley to Gun Hill, passing the row of old brass cannons that faced out to sea, and heading down onto the beach where the sand dunes began.

The sky was blue, and the sun was clear and bright, and a fresh breeze blew the waves into foam-topped breakers. 'I can't believe it's such a lovely day,' said Lucy. 'Especially after the foul weather we had last night.'

'Sherlock and I love coming here in winter,' said Charlie. 'Dogs aren't allowed on the beach in the summer, so it's the best time of year for us.'

Sherlock was already scampering across the dunes, his doggy ears inside out in the wind. He kept his nose close to the ground for the scent of seagulls. Sherlock regarded seagulls as the finest sport a dog could get. He would chase them whenever he got the opportunity, and Charlie would get angry and try to stop him whenever he did. Seagulls were about the only thing that Sherlock and Charlie ever disagreed on.

The walk along the sand dunes was bright and refreshing, even though Max complained continuously that his electric skateboard didn't work on the sand and that it was too heavy to be carrying all this way. 'I mean, what is the point,' he said for the tenth time, 'of having one of the most advanced forms of transport known to man if you have to pick it up and stuff it under your arm?'

'Stop moaning,' said Lucy. 'We're nearly there.'

At the southern end of the dunes, they passed the summer campsites, now empty and deserted, and reached the point where the River Blyth met the coastline. At the mouth of the harbour, an old jetty stuck out into the sea like a concrete and steel finger, and the wind howled across the empty car park. But just as Lucy had predicted, a blue-painted kiosk was open for business, offering teas, coffees, milkshakes, scones and ... *ice creams*.

Lucy ran over to the kiosk and returned a few moments later with four vanilla cones, all sprouting chocolate flakes.

'You are nuts, Lucy Yeung,' said Max. 'It's the middle of December.'

'I'll eat yours if you don't want it.' Joe laughed. He had already taken a huge mouthful.

'Don't worry,' said Max with a grin. 'I'll force it down. Thanks, Luce.'

As well as the ice creams, Lucy had also bought a packet of dog biscuits for Sherlock, which she handed to Charlie. 'Thank you,' said Charlie as she took the packet. 'It's very good of you to think of Sherlock too.'

Lucy shrugged. 'Of course,' she said. 'He's one of the gang too.'

'So, we're a gang now?' said Joe, brightening.

Max shrugged. 'I guess so,' he said. 'But if anyone makes me walk much further today, I'm putting in for a transfer.'

For a while, nobody spoke as they strolled along the bank, licking their ice creams. They passed shuttered booths that offered boat trips to the tourists in summer, fishermen's huts with corrugated tin roofs, rusty winches, and empty oil drums collecting rainwater.

A line of grey gulls stood expectantly on the wooden pilings where the fishing vessels tied up, hoping for a dropped fish. Sherlock gave them a sideways glance but quickly returned his attention to the packet of dog biscuits in Charlie's hand. The seagulls could wait for now.

The three of them sat on some wooden railings overlooking a concrete slipway while they finished their cones. Charlie broke the biscuits into smaller pieces and handed them around so they could take turns feeding Sherlock, an arrangement that suited Sherlock very well.

Their perch gave them a view across the river to Walberswick and the flat marshlands, criss-crossed with hedgerows, long grasses and purple-headed rushes. The harbour itself was bleak and deserted. Many of the larger boats had been taken out of the water for the winter and raised up on wooden blocks with black tarpaulins lashed tightly across their upper decks.

Max looked along the harbour front at a spot where a scruffy man was loading boxes into a large rubber dinghy. A short distance away, a motorbike had pulled up close to the quayside. As soon as the scruffy man saw the motorbike, he stopped what he was doing and scowled.

'What do you suppose is going on over there?'

said Max. 'It looks like those two are pretty annoyed with each other.'

The children could not hear clearly what was being said, but the odd words reached them above the noise of the wind. 'Where were you? Last night... waiting...' growled the scruffy man. He jabbed an accusing finger at the motorcyclist when he spoke. 'Can't afford any more of your mess-ups...'

The motorcyclist seemed to be quite agitated too. He was still wearing his helmet, so they could not hear what he was saying clearly, but he shrugged his shoulders and held out his hands, palms upwards in an 'it's not my fault' sort of gesture.

The scruffy man was beginning to get really angry now. He shouted something more loudly, but Sherlock chose that moment to begin barking, and the words were lost. The instant the little dog had seen the two men, his ears had gone back and he had begun to growl. Now he was barking like a dog twice his size.

'Be quiet, Sherlock,' hissed Charlie. 'We're trying to hear.' But even though Charlie grabbed him firmly by the collar, Sherlock would not stop barking, and they could hear no more of what was being said.

Worse still, the noise had attracted the attention of the two men, who were now staring in their direction. The scruffy man scowled at the children and then beckoned the motorcyclist into a nearby boat shed and out of sight.

'They looked pretty suspicious if you ask me,' said Joe.

'Well, Sherlock certainly didn't like either of them,' said Charlie. 'And he's *always* a good judge of character.'

'I think Sherlock might be right,' said Max thoughtfully. 'Did you notice the man on the motorcycle had a piece torn out of his jeans in exactly the spot where Sherlock ripped the Spectre's trousers last night?'

The others stared at Max in amazement. 'I didn't notice that,' said Lucy. 'How on earth did you manage to see something so tiny?'

Max smirked. 'I like to think of myself as a details man.'

'You don't think that man's a ghost, do you?' asked Joe. 'He looked real enough to me.'

'Don't be ridiculous,' said Max. 'Of course he's not a ghost. But I think he might have been pretending to be one last night. And Sherlock obviously thinks so too.'

'But why would anyone stand on a beach and pretend to be a ghost?' asked Charlie. 'That makes no sense at all.'

'Unless he was up to no good,' said Joe. 'Perhaps he'd also heard the story of the fisherman and the mermaid, and he thought it would be a good way to scare people away. Maybe he really is a wrecker after all?'

'Captain Tom said there were no wreckers in these parts,' said Lucy. 'It must be something else.'

'But what?' said Joe.

Before anyone could offer an idea about what the man had been doing, they were interrupted by a thin, nasally voice coming from behind them. 'And what exactly are you four up to?'

The children all jumped with surprise. They had been so intent on watching the two men that they had not noticed someone approaching them from behind. They turned around to see a pinched man wearing a naval uniform. His peaked white cap was pulled so low that he had to peer down his nose to see them properly.

The man's uniform might once have been impressive. It had a double-breasted jacket and large buttons that looked like chocolate coins covered in gold foil. But the jacket was several sizes too large for him, and the trousers were spotted with grease. It looked like something he had bought in a second-hand store.

'Who are you?' said Max.

'Who am I?' repeated the man incredulously, as though everyone ought to know who he was. 'I'll tell you who I am, young man.' He leaned in, giving Max a whiff of his eggy breath. 'I am none other than the Queen's Harbour Master. Creech is the name. Walter Creech.'

Mr Creech's beady eyes roamed over the children as he curled his lip. Joe noticed that he had a postage-stamp-sized patch of hair beneath his nose that twitched every time he talked.

'I'll have you know that I have the power to arrest miscreants within this vicinity.'

'Mis-what?' said Joe with a frown.

'It means troublemakers,' said Mr Creech, baring

his yellow teeth as he spoke. 'Like you lot.'

'But we haven't done anything,' said Lucy. 'We just came here to eat our ice creams.'

'Don't give me that!' snapped Mr Creech. 'I saw you eyeing up those boat sheds. You've come here to steal something, I bet. I'm going to call your parents.' He pulled out a clipboard from behind his back. 'Right then, names and addresses, please.'

Lucy was incensed. 'Now look here!' She drew herself up to her full height, which was almost as tall as Mr Creech, and looked him straight in the eye. 'We don't have to give you our names and addresses,' she said. 'We've as much right to be here as anyone else.'

'Hang on a minute,' said Mr Creech, looking past Lucy. He had caught sight of Charlie standing at the back of the group. 'I know you! You're the one who owns that vicious little dog.'

Sherlock could not understand anything that was being said, but he didn't like Mr Creech's tone

one little bit. He bared his teeth at the Harbour Master and barked. The effect on Mr Creech was immediate. His eyes widened with fear, and he jumped behind Lucy, holding out his clipboard in front of him like a shield. 'Keep that beast away from me. He went for me last summer. He's vicious, he is.'

Charlie grabbed Sherlock's collar and scowled at Mr Creech. 'He's not vicious,' she said. 'You just startled him because you threw cold water on him.'

Mr Creech scowled. 'Don't think I don't know who you are, young lady,' he said. 'You're that Charlotte Wells with the mother who lets you run wild. I've a good mind to call the police and have that dog put down.'

'No!' Charlie gasped in horror. She shrank back from Mr Creech, and her face turned as pale as death. 'You can't do that!' she cried. 'Sherlock's done you no harm. He, he...'

Mr Creech looked very pleased with himself,

and a nasty smile had spread across his face. Then Max stepped forward and tapped him on the shoulder.

'As I understand it, Mr Creech,' he said, 'the Harbour Master is responsible for the safety of all vessels while they are in the harbour. Isn't that true?'

Mr Creech looked down his nose at Max. The postage-stamp moustache twitched in an irritated fashion. 'More or less,' he said cautiously.

'Well,' said Max, 'it looks to me like there's a boat over there with a loose tarpaulin flapping in the breeze. That could cause a nasty accident if someone doesn't do something about it.'

The tiny moustache twitched back and forth like a dancing caterpillar under Mr Creech's nose. 'Now look here, you little squirt—' he began.

'And furthermore,' said Max, pointing to a row of oil tanks beside a boat shed, 'one of those oil tanks is dripping fuel oil, which constitutes an environmental and a fire hazard.' Max adopted a pained expression. 'I'd hate to have to tell the authorities that the Harbour Master isn't doing his job properly.'

'What?' Mr Creech looked startled. His eyes darted from the loose tarpaulin to the dripping oil tank and back again. 'Well... I-I was just about to do something about those things,' he stammered. 'But I got distracted by you lot.' He began to back away, holding out the clipboard in front of him as he went. 'Anyway, I don't have time to stand here talking to kids all day. I've got work to do. Just mind you don't get up to any more mischief.'

He continued to back away until he was sure he was a safe distance from Sherlock. Then, with as much dignity as he could muster, he straightened his jacket and marched away stiffly. Lucy, Joe and Charlie watched him go with open mouths.

'Max,' gasped Lucy when he had gone, 'that was amazing!'

Max shrugged. 'My dad says you should always

stand up to bullies,' he said. Then he sighed. 'I only wish I could get it to work on Toby Watts.'

'Well, I think you did great,' said Joe admiringly. 'Did you see the way Creech went slinking off with his tail between his legs?'

'Thank you, Max,' said Charlie quietly. She still looked pale, but she managed a small smile. 'I'd die if someone tried to take Sherlock away from me.'

'Well, nobody's going to do that,' said Lucy. 'At least not while we're your friends. We can fight off Harbour Masters and ghosts alike.'

'Speaking of our ghost,' said Max, 'it looks like he's on the move.'

While they had been dealing with Mr Creech, the two men had emerged from the boat shed. The motorcyclist quickly mounted his motorbike and roared away in a cloud of blue smoke. The scruffy man scowled at them from a distance and then walked to his dinghy. In just a few moments he had started the outboard engine and was steering away from the dockside.

'Where's he going in such a tiny boat?' said Lucy. 'It's not big enough to get very far.'

'My guess is he's heading for that yacht out there,' said Max, pointing.

About a mile offshore they could see a large yacht at anchor. It was white and sleek with furled sails and wooden decks. They watched the little dinghy chugging towards the yacht until it drew alongside. A second person appeared on the deck to help tie up the dinghy, but they were too far away to get a clear view of what the other man looked like.

'Do you think the person we saw last night was signalling to the people on that yacht?' said Joe.

'Why would he do that?' said Lucy. 'They could just bring the boat into the harbour and talk to him any time they want to. That doesn't make much sense.'

'Unless they wanted to bring something ashore without being seen,' said Max. 'Something they didn't want the harbour authorities to know about.'

'You mean they might be smugglers?' asked Charlie breathlessly. The word hung in the air, conjuring images in the children's heads of pirates and wooden chests filled with pearls and gold pieces.

Lucy frowned. 'What would they be smuggling?'

'Barrels of rum,' said Joe quickly. 'And tobacco and spices and fine silks. I read all about it in a book on pirates.'

'That was hundreds of years ago,' said Max. 'You can buy all those things in the shops now. They must be smuggling something else. But what?'

'Well, we've got no way of finding out,' said Lucy. She pointed out to sea. 'They're out there, and we're stuck here. It's not like we've got a boat and can just sail over there and say, "Excuse me, but could you tell us what you're smuggling, please?"'

The others laughed, but Joe looked serious.

'I've got a boat,' he said suddenly.

Lucy, Max and Charlie turned to look at him. 'Do you mean some radio-controlled toy that your dad bought for you?' said Charlie. 'Be serious, Joe.'

'I am being serious,' insisted Joe. 'I *have* got a boat. Well, it's my dad's, really. He bought a motorboat at the same time as he bought the beach hut. He had some idea that we were all going to spend all our summers out on the sea. But he's never here, and my mum gets seasick. So, most of the time it just sits idle.'

'Where is it?' said Lucy.

'In a private boathouse, just up there,' said Joe, pointing. 'We could take it out to have a look at that big yacht and see if we can find any clues – my dad won't mind. Besides, it would be just like being real detectives or secret agents.'

Charlie snorted. 'You watch too many movies,' she said. 'We can't sail up to them in broad daylight. They'd see us coming for miles.'

'We could go tonight, after dark,' said Joe excitedly. 'Then when we get close to the yacht, we can turn off the engine and row the last bit so they don't hear us.'

'I don't know about that,' said Lucy. 'Taking out a motorboat at night sounds pretty dangerous.'

'Dad made sure I had the safety training when he bought the boat,' said Joe. 'He thought it would be a good idea. And we've got all the safety equipment. We'll be perfectly safe, I promise.' He looked at them all pleadingly. 'Come on, it'll be fun.'

They fell silent while they contemplated the prospect of a midnight motorboat ride to investigate the possible smugglers. It certainly sounded pretty exciting.

'Alright,' said Lucy eventually. 'I guess it can't do any harm to go and have a *little* look. What's the worst that can happen?'

'Great!' said Joe, thumping his fist into his palm. 'I'll go home and get the keys and meet you here this evening. Quick, everyone give me your phone numbers so I can let you know when I'm on my way.'

They pulled out their phones and exchanged numbers. 'Good,' said Joe when they were done. 'I'll head down here straight after dinner. I'll drop you all a message when I'm on my way.'

Lucy bit her lip. 'Joe, are you absolutely sure your parents won't mind us taking their boat?' she said.

Joe had already started to sprint away. He turned and called back over his shoulder. 'Of course they won't,' he said. 'Just stop worrying. You can *trust* me.'

9

THE *SEA QUEEN*

That evening they met again on the harbour front, under cover of darkness. Max rolled up on his electric skateboard and found Lucy, Charlie and Sherlock waiting for him.

'So, where's Joe?' he said as he glided to a halt. 'He messaged me to say he was on his way, but that was ages ago. He hasn't stood us up, has he?'

'I wouldn't put it past him,' said Charlie. She shivered and pulled her fleecy jacket tightly around herself. Now that the sun was gone, the night air was bitter, and the moon cast a soft silver light behind thin clouds.

Lucy looked curiously at the large backpack

that Max was carrying. It looked full of something very heavy. 'What have you got in there?' she asked.

Max tapped the side of his nose. 'Just a few bits and pieces from the stockroom,' he said. 'Stuff every modern detective needs, you'll see.'

Just then, Joe arrived. He looked like he had run all the way from his house. He was pink in the face, and his eyes were gleaming with excitement.

'Sorry I'm late,' he gasped. 'I had to wait for Mum to go out before I could leave. She thinks I'm staying in to do my homework.'

'Did you get the keys?' asked Max expectantly.

Joe fished in his pocket and pulled out a bunch of keys that gleamed softly in the moonlight. 'Come on,' he said. 'The boat shed's just up here.'

He led them past working fishing boats that had been secured for the night and rows of gulls hunched down on the boat shed roofs. They travelled in a line, nobody speaking as they moved swiftly through the boatyards, keeping to the grass verges to deaden the sound of their footfalls and feeling more like secret agents with every step. Even Sherlock seemed to know that he was meant to be quiet as he snuffled along at Charlie's heels.

About halfway along the harbour front they passed by the Harbour Master's office, a stern black shed bristling with warning signs and a notice board listing the harbour regulations. The office windows were dark.

'That means that Creech is out on his rounds,' said Joe. 'We'll have to keep an eye out for him.'

A little way beyond the Harbour Master's office, a small boathouse with green-painted doors lay close to the water. A concrete slipway led from the boathouse to allow a boat to be wheeled down to the water's edge. 'It's in here,' said Joe. There was a heavy padlock on the door, and Joe fumbled with the keys, trying several in the lock without success. The others formed a tight huddle behind him, peering over his shoulder and buzzing with excitement.

'Can't you get a move on?' hissed Max. 'Someone will see us.'

'I'm going as quick as I can,' snapped Joe. 'Perhaps if you all stop crowding me.'

'What about that key?' asked Lucy. 'It looks like it might fit.'

'Quiet!' hissed Charlie from the back. 'There's someone coming.'

Everyone stopped talking and held their breath. The sound of steady footsteps could be heard crunching along the gravel path towards them.

Charlie stuck her head around the side of the shed to take a look. The wide cone of a torch beam was swinging from side to side as it came along the path. Then she saw a skinny shadow in a peaked cap, holding the torch.

'It's Creech!' she hissed. 'And he's coming this way!'

They all slipped into the shadows and pressed tightly against the doors of the boathouse, hoping that Creech wouldn't catch sight of them. The footsteps came closer and closer until they were level with the boathouse, and then, horror of horrors, they stopped. Max caught Lucy's wide-eyed expression as the torch beam shone along the side of the boathouse and illuminated the concrete slipway barely a metre from where they were hiding.

'Who's there?' came Creech's nasally voice. 'Come on. I know there's someone down there.'

Max's mouth went dry, and his heart thumped like a rubber mallet in his chest. He felt sure that Creech must be able to hear it. Lucy clamped a hand across her own mouth to stop herself from making a noise, and Joe squeezed his eyes tight shut as though that might keep him hidden. Charlie crouched in front of Sherlock and raised a warning finger. The little dog seemed to understand and kept dead still.

Creech's footsteps started down the slipway towards their hiding place. But, just when they felt sure they would be discovered, a gull that had been roosting on a piling stirred itself and took to the air with a wheezy cry.

There was a startled shout from Creech as the bird took off, and he whirled around, tracking the bird with his torch. Then he grunted and muttered something under his breath. The torch snapped off, and a moment later, they heard his footsteps fading back down the gravel path.

The children let out a collective sigh of relief. 'That was too close for comfort,' gasped Joe.

'Hurry up and get this door open before he decides to come back,' hissed Max.

Joe fumbled with the keys again, and, this time,

he got lucky. The padlock sprang open, and Joe hauled open the wooden doors. He fished a torch from his pocket and shone it inside the shed, and the children all gasped with delight.

Standing inside the shed was a small motorboat on a wheeled trailer. The boat was made of wood the colour of leather and honey, and there were two rows of seats upholstered in a shiny red. There was a white steering wheel and a tiny flagpole at the back. Gold lettering on the front of the boat spelled out the name *Sea Queen*.

'Awesome!' said Max.

'It's beautiful!' said Lucy in a hushed voice.

'She's a 1961 Chris-Craft Capri,' said Joe proudly. 'My dad said he paid an arm and a leg for it.'

'I'm surprised your dad's got any arms and legs left,' said Charlie.

Max ran his fingers along the smooth wood. It felt warm to the touch, like a living thing. 'Are you sure you know how to drive this?'

'Of course,' said Joe. 'I told you, my dad made

me do all the safety training. The weather forecast is fine, and there's fuel in the engine. There's life jackets under the seats, and I've got everything else we need right here.' He pulled off his own rucksack and threw it into the back of the boat. 'There's an air horn, some whistles, a torch, a first aid kit and a couple of flares.

Lucy grinned. 'You weren't kidding,' she said. 'You really have done the safety training, haven't you?'

Joe flushed with pride. 'You can't be too careful at sea,' he said. 'Now help me get her down to the water.'

Together they picked up the front of the trailer and wheeled the boat gently down the slipway to the river. While Max held the mooring rope, the others pushed the trailer into the water until the boat floated free. They were wet up to their knees, but nobody cared. They were all too eager to get started.

While Joe locked up the boathouse again, the

others climbed into the boat and settled on the comfy red seats. It took a while for Charlie to lift Sherlock inside. 'Blimey, Sherlock. You really are heavy for such a small dog,' she said as she handed him up to Max.

At last, they were all on board and ready to leave. Joe sat in the driver's seat with Lucy next to him while Charlie and Max sat in the back with Sherlock between them. Joe made them all put on their life jackets and made a great show of checking that they were fastened correctly. There was even a dog-sized life vest for Sherlock, which he sniffed at dubiously while Charlie put it on.

'If I start the engine, old Creech will hear it immediately,' said Joe. 'We'll have to paddle quietly out of the harbour.'

He took two paddles from beneath the seat and handed one to Lucy, and together they dipped them into the water and began to paddle the boat. It took some time to get out to the middle of the river, but as soon as they did, the current began to carry them quite rapidly.

'It's a good job the tide's on the way out,' said Joe. 'Otherwise we'd never be able to paddle against the current.'

The river took them quite swiftly now, and Joe and Lucy only needed to dip the paddles into the water occasionally to keep the *Sea Queen* in the middle of the flow. They fell silent as they passed the illuminated windows of the Harbour Master's office. 'Creech must have gone inside for the evening,' said Joe. 'We'll be fine now.'

In the back seat, Max relaxed and leaned back as he took a deep lungful of the sea air. There was something about being on a boat, he decided, that just made everything feel more adventurous. Then the boat lurched, and Max sat up with a start.

When they reached the mouth of the harbour, the waves caught the little boat, slapping against the wooden hull and tossing it up and down like a rocking horse. Joe turned on the ignition and pressed the starter button. There was a slow whirring noise from the back of the boat that sounded like a creature in pain. Frowning, he tried again, with the same result.

'What's up?' asked Max. The motion of the waves was starting to make him feel seasick.

'Nothing to worry about,' said Joe. 'The battery's a bit flat, that's all. It might take a moment to get going.'

'Didn't you think to check it before we left?' hissed Charlie from the back.

'Well, I couldn't very well start the engine with Creech snooping around, could I?' snapped Joe.

'Can you stop it swaying about so much?' said Max. He was feeling decidedly queasy now and regretting the third helping of his mum's curry that he'd eaten before he left home.

Lucy glanced anxiously over her shoulder. The current had carried them some distance offshore. 'Joe, what if you can't get it started?' she asked. 'Will we be able to get back?'

Joe didn't answer, but he was now starting to look worried. He stared at the ignition switch and pressed repeatedly on the starter button. Suddenly, the engine coughed and sprang to life. There was a brief roar and a rush of petrol fumes, and the engine settled to a steady purr.

Everybody breathed a sigh of relief, and Joe broke out in a huge grin. 'I knew it!' he cried. 'I knew there was nothing to worry about.'

Now that the engine was running, Joe pushed on the throttle and steered the boat into the waves. The boat began to skip lightly between the peaks, and Max's queasiness began to recede. Sherlock put his paws up on the seat between Joe and Lucy and let his ears stream backwards in the breeze. Even Charlie was smiling.

'This is brilliant, Joe,' said Lucy. 'I can't understand why your mum doesn't like boats.'

'She likes them well enough when she goes on holiday to places like Italy,' said Joe. 'But she doesn't really like anything about Southwold.'

'Well, I think this is the best way to travel, ever,' said Max. 'Do you think we could get all the way to France in this thing?'

'Not without a lot more petrol,' said Joe.

'I'd settle for just getting to that yacht and back without Joe's boat conking out on us again,' said Charlie.

Joe steered steadily towards the yacht, and they could now see how big it was. 'She's a beauty,' said Joe as they drew nearer. 'She's easily an eighty-footer. She could probably sail halfway around the world if she wanted to.'

They could see that the yacht was securely anchored, and the rubber dinghy they had seen earlier was now tied up on a long rope behind it. There was no sign of anyone on the deck, but there were lights inside the cabin, and one of the portholes in the side of the boat was open. 'Better cut the engine before they hear us,' said Max.

Joe turned off the engine, and the little boat fell quiet. As soon as the noise died away, they heard the sound of loud music coming from inside the boat. 'Well, they're definitely home,' said Max. 'Can you get us any closer?'

'Grab the paddle, Lucy,' said Joe. 'Let's go carefully, though. If they spot us, we'll have to pretend that we're just out on a night-time fishing trip.'

'Yeah, because we all look just like fishermen,' said Charlie sarcastically.

Joe ignored her and picked up his own paddle. He and Lucy tried to propel them forwards without making too much sound, but as they drew closer, it was obvious that the music inside the yacht was too loud for anyone to hear what was going on outside.

Joe guided them expertly alongside the yacht, not touching, but close enough that they could look up at the open porthole. The sound of muffled voices was coming from within, but they couldn't make out what was being said over the noise of the music.

'Now what?' asked Charlie. 'We're not going to find out anything like this. We might as well turn around and go back before someone spots us.'

Joe opened his mouth to reply, but, before he could speak, the music snapped off, and there was silence apart from the slapping of the waves.

'Quiet,' hissed Lucy. 'If we make a noise now, we'll be rumbled!'

10

SMUGGLERS!

The children stared at each other in horror as their boat bobbed next to the yacht. Max could see that Lucy was right. Now that the music had stopped, the slightest noise would give them away. He was about to signal to Joe that they should start using the paddles to move away as quietly as possible when they heard voices talking inside the yacht again. This time they could hear what was being said very clearly.

'Oi!' said an angry voice. 'I was listening to that.' The voice was rough and filled with menace, and Max guessed it belonged to the scruffy man they had seen in the dinghy.

'You call that music, Sharkey?' said a second man. 'That's just a horrible noise. Besides, I don't pay you good money to lie around on my boat while there's work to be done.'

'I've done all my work,' said the man called Sharkey. 'I fetched the supplies from the harbour, and I washed the decks, like you asked. Aren't I entitled to a bit of peace for five minutes?'

'You're forgetting that we've still got merchandise to be delivered,' the other voice snapped. 'Did you speak to that friend of yours? What happened to him last night? He was supposed to meet us. You told me he was reliable.'

'I saw him earlier while I was out getting supplies,' said Sharkey. 'He said it wasn't his fault.' He sounded apologetic. 'He waited for us on the sea wall at the right time, but he got attacked by a dog.'

'A dog?'

'He said it was massive,' replied Sharkey. 'A Great Dane or an Alsatian or something. He was lucky to get away with his life.'

Outside in the darkness, the four children looked at each other and then at Sherlock. It was difficult to see how anyone could mistake him for a Great Dane.

'Well, it's not good enough!' snapped the other man. 'I need to offload that merchandise. The moon's too bright to try again right now, but as soon as we get a cloudy night, I want it off my boat. And no mess-ups this time!' His voice turned icy cold. 'Otherwise you'll have bodies to dispose of.'

Joe gasped and clamped a hand across his mouth to stop himself from making any noises. The others looked at each other, wide-eyed with terror.

Bodies! thought Max. The man was actually talking about disposing of bodies. His head swam.

With a panicked expression, Joe grabbed the paddle and signalled to Lucy to do the same. Trying to avoid making a splash, they paddled the

Sea Queen backwards through the water until they were several metres away from the yacht.

'Wait, wait,' said Max in a whisper. 'Where are we going?'

'Away from here,' hissed Joe. 'As fast as we can. Didn't you hear what that guy said? They're smuggling something, and they're talking about disposing of bodies too. They're not just smugglers, Max, they're murderers! We have to go to the police.'

'And tell them what?' said Max. 'We need evidence if we're ever going to prove that.'

'What are you suggesting?' asked Lucy.

'We need to find out when they're going to try to bring that merchandise ashore again,' said Max. 'Then we can tell the police, and they can catch them red-handed.'

'How are we going to do that?' asked Charlie. 'We can't very well watch their boat every night, can we?'

'Perhaps we can,' said Max, with a smile. He

began to rummage in his backpack. 'I've got something in here that might help.' He pulled out a device about the size of a tin of beans. There was a small circuit board connected to a battery and an old-style mobile phone. The whole collection of items was stuck together with thick wrappings of black insulating tape.

'What on earth is that?' asked Charlie. 'It looks like a bomb!'

'Home-made tracking device,' said Max proudly. 'The mobile phone picks up the GPS signal, and the circuit board's been modified to run the tracking software. The battery should be good for about a week.' He grinned as he held the device in his hand. 'I can track the whole thing from the computer in my bedroom. If we hide it in that dinghy, I'll know as soon as they head towards the shore.'

The others stared at the device in Max's hand. 'I have no idea what any of that means,' said Charlie, 'but if that thing does what you say it will, then you're a genius.'

'It's incredible,' said Joe. 'It really will be like being secret agents. How long will it take to plant it?'

'A few seconds,' said Max. 'Bring us a bit closer to the dinghy. And keep the noise down.'

Joe and Lucy picked up the paddles again and rowed them closer to the rubber dinghy. The boat was tied to a long rope strung out at the back of the yacht, and it was easy to pull it alongside without alerting anyone inside as to what was happening.

Lucy kept an anxious eye on the yacht as Max carefully threw his leg over the side of the *Sea Queen* and stepped down into the dinghy. The rubber boat rocked violently, and Max had to bend his knees to avoid being thrown into the water. He crept to the back of the boat and reached under the dinghy's bench seat. He took out some old rags to make some space and then placed his device under the seat, remembering to switch it on first. After he had replaced the rags, he leaned back to admire his handiwork.

'Perfect,' he said. 'No one will suspect a thing.'

'Okay, then,' said Joe. 'Get back in here, quick.'

Max turned to leave but then paused. 'Wait a minute,' he said. A splash of colour in the front of the boat had caught his eye. There was something small and bright green lodged in a crevice beneath one of the front seats.

Watching from the boat, Sherlock's ears went back, and he let out a low growl. 'Max!' said Lucy. 'What are you doing now? We need to get out of here. Now!'

'One second,' said Max. He bent down to retrieve the strange item and examined it in the half-light. Then he slipped it into his pocket. 'Okay,' he said. 'I'm ready. Let's go.'

He was halfway back inside the motorboat with

one leg over the side when the dark sea turned suddenly to daylight, and an angry shout came from the direction of the yacht.

'What the blazes do you think you're doing on my boat!' Two strong floodlights were turned on the *Sea Queen*.

'Thieves!' shouted the angry voice. 'Sharkey, stop them!'

Max's mouth went dry and his legs felt wobbly. He looked around at his friends and saw they were all wearing the same terrified expressions. Even Sherlock looked afraid. The little dog's ears had folded back, and he crouched down low in the seat beside Charlie. Max wondered if there was still time to start the boat and get away, but one look at Joe told him it was impossible.

'Bring them alongside,' barked the man. 'We'll show them what we do to thieves and vandals.'

A moment later, a long boat hook connected with the front of the *Sea Queen*, making a large scratch on the wood panelling as the motorboat was dragged towards the yacht. Max looked around in horror, but there was no escape.

They had been caught by the smugglers!

11

DISGRACED!

Sharkey pulled the *Sea Queen* alongside the yacht and tied it up while the other man barked orders at them. 'All of you, get out of that boat and climb up here on the deck.'

The man was stout and wore an expensive blazer with a nautical cap. He was very red in the face and he had jowls that wobbled when he spoke. When they were all lined up before him, he glared at them while Sharkey stood behind, holding the boat hook. 'My name is Quentin De Havilland,' he said with an angry shake of his jowls. 'I'll have you know I'm a very important man in these parts, and I don't take kindly to young criminals trying to steal my property.'

'W-we're not,' stammered Joe. 'I m-mean we weren't. We were just... er...' Joe realised he had no idea how he was going to finish his sentence.

'What Joe means to say,' said Max quickly, 'is that we were just out fishing, but then we broke down.'

'A likely story,' fumed De Havilland. 'So how do you explain being in my dinghy? Come on, own up. You were trying to steal it, weren't you?' While he was speaking, his face became redder and redder until he looked like an overinflated party balloon that was ready to pop.

Sharkey looked at the children through narrowed eyes. 'I know this lot,' he said. 'They were the ones who were watching me and Dean down at the harbour. I recognise that little rat of a dog.' He pointed at Sherlock, who growled and bared his teeth in response to the insult. Charlie kept a tight grip on his collar.

'Keep that animal under control,' snapped De

Havilland. 'He's a menace.'

'Hey,' said Sharkey suddenly. 'You don't suppose they were listening, do you?' He nodded meaningfully to De Havilland. 'When you and me were discussing *business*?'

De Havilland frowned and looked at the children thoughtfully. 'How long were you all snooping around outside my yacht? Tell me the truth now.'

'We weren't,' said Joe quickly. 'Snooping, I mean.'

'We'd only just arrived when you came out and saw us,' said Lucy.

'Why?' said Max. 'Did we miss anything interesting?' He regretted his words almost as soon as he said them.

'Less of your cheek, lad,' said De Havilland, turning several shades redder. Then he turned to Sharkey. 'Get the dinghy ready. We'll hand them over to the harbour authorities and let the police deal with them.'

The children gasped. 'The police?' cried Lucy.

'But you can't. I've never been in trouble with the police before.'

'My mum will kill me,' said Max. 'Dad got a parking ticket once, and she never let him hear the end of it.'

Joe and Charlie said nothing. They just looked down at their feet.

A nasty smile crept across De Havilland's face. 'How unfortunate for you all,' he said. 'Perhaps that will teach you a lesson: crime doesn't pay.'

'We're not the ones who are the criminals,' muttered Joe.

'What did you say?' De Havilland shot Joe a glare.

'What Joe meant to say,' said Lucy, 'is that none of us are criminals. If you just let us go, we'll go straight home, and we won't bother you again.'

But it was no use. The more they pleaded not to be taken to the police, the more De Havilland seemed to enjoy the prospect of doing exactly that. Sharkey pulled the rubber dinghy alongside, and De Havilland ordered them all to climb into it. Then, with Sharkey driving, they started back towards the harbour, towing the *Sea Queen* behind them.

'What are we going to do?' asked Joe miserably as they made the journey. 'I'm going to be grounded until I'm middle-aged.'

'The one thing we can't do is tell the truth,' said Max. He kept his voice down so that the two men could not hear him over the sound of the dinghy's outboard motor.

'What do you mean?' asked Lucy. 'Surely you're not suggesting we lie to the police?'

'If we tell the police that these men are smugglers, they'll never believe us,' said Max. 'They'll just think we're making it up to avoid getting into trouble. And, what's worse, if these guys realise that we suspect them, then they'll just hide the evidence. The police will never catch them after that.'

'He's right,' said Charlie. 'I don't know what

they're smuggling, but they're definitely up to no good. Sherlock doesn't like them one bit, and he's never wrong about people. Until we've got some better evidence, we have to keep quiet about what we know, or they'll get away scot-free.'

'Stop talking back there,' growled Sharkey.

The four children sat in silence for the rest of the journey. As the boat ploughed through the waves towards the harbour, all of them were thinking the same thing. They were most definitely in serious trouble now.

When they arrived, De Havilland marched them triumphantly into the Harbour Master's office, with Sharkey following close behind. Creech was sitting behind his desk, eating egg sandwiches and drinking tea from a tartan-patterned thermos flask. He looked up when they entered, and his mouth dropped open in surprise, giving them all a view of a half-chewed egg sandwich. As soon as Creech saw De Havilland, he jumped up from behind his desk.

'Mr De Havilland, sir,' he said in a fawning voice. 'What an unexpected pleasure. To what do we owe the honour of your presence?' He rubbed his hands together when he spoke, and a thin toady smile spread across his face.

When De Havilland explained why he was there, the Harbour Master's eyes widened with horror. He shook his head in disbelief and made disapproving noises. 'Tried to steal your boat, you say?' he said in an outraged tone. 'I knew they were trouble the moment I clapped eyes on them. Chased them out of my harbour this very afternoon, I did. Oh, you did the right thing bringing them to me, Mr De Havilland. I'll call the police immediately.'

Creech's words made the children's hearts sink. Max wondered idly whether they served Christmas dinner in prison. While Creech telephoned for the police, Sharkey disappeared outside, seemingly anxious to be somewhere else when they arrived. Mr De Havilland took a seat in the corner, and

Creech returned to his sandwiches, pausing occasionally to look up at the children and smirk in a very self-satisfied sort of way.

Two police officers arrived. One went outside to inspect the rubber dinghy and see if any damage had been done, while a female officer began to question the children.

It took a long time to tell their stories. The police officer looked weary, like someone who has far more important things to do than deal with four children who had been caught creeping about on someone else's boat. She insisted on writing everything down very slowly in her notebook. While she wrote, she kept pausing to lick the end of her pencil, which Max thought was probably very unhygienic.

When she had finished writing, she read through her notes, frowning at the pages while the children stood in a line in front of the desk, looking shamefaced and miserable. 'So,' she said when she had finished, 'tell me again what happened.'

The children groaned. 'We've already explained it...' said Lucy.

'At least three times now,' added Joe.

The police officer looked down at her notebook and frowned. 'Yes, you did,' she said. 'The only trouble is your stories don't add up. You said you were out night fishing, but none of you has any fishing equipment. You said your engine cut out, but my officer could find nothing wrong with your boat. And you had no explanation at all for why you were found on board Mr De Havilland's dinghy.'

'It's like I told you,' said Max. 'It looked like it was coming untied. I was just trying to make sure it was properly secure.' Max winced when he told the lie. He was aware of how unbelievable their story sounded, but they had all agreed they could not tell the truth about what had happened. Not yet.

The police officer took off her glasses and rubbed her face while Max wondered how many times she would go on asking the same questions. He was just thinking how tired he felt and how much he wanted to be at home in his bed when the door opened and Joe's mother walked in.

Penelope Carter had the sort of face that naturally fell into a suspicious frown. She scanned the room until her gaze settled on Joe, then descended on her son like an angry bird. 'Joseph Carter! What *have* you been up to? And who are all these *people*?'

She looked at Lucy, Max and Charlie as though she had found them living underneath her bins and was thinking of spraying them with disinfectant. Then she turned back to her son. 'I was at a dinner party with the Hamilton-Browns when I got a call from the police. The *police*, Joseph. I could have *died* of embarrassment.'

'Perhaps I could be of some assistance, madam,' said Creech, with an oily smile. 'The name's Creech. I am the Queen's Harbour Master here, and it's my responsibility to—'

Mrs Carter pushed past Creech and approached the police officer sitting behind the desk. She turned on a smile that glowed as though someone had thrown a switch. 'Officer,' she gushed. 'Penelope Carter. Perhaps you could tell me what my son is supposed to have done? I'm sure there's a simple explanation, but if there's any damage,

I'd be only too happy to pay...' She began to open her handbag.

The police officer held up her hand. 'That won't be necessary, Mrs Carter,' he said. 'No damage as far as we can see. It seems your son took his friends out in your motorboat for a bit of a joyride.'

'The motorboat!' she whirled around and fixed her son with a glare that felt to Joe like being under a magnifying glass in the sun. 'How many times have we told you, Joe? You are *not* to take that boat without permission.' The other children stared at Joe in disbelief.

'So,' said Mrs Carter, turning her smile back on the police officer. 'What will happen to Joe now?'

The officer shrugged. 'Well, that's very much up to Mr De Havilland, madam.'

Mrs Carter turned and caught sight of De Havilland for the first time. For a moment her eyes widened in surprise; then the smile flicked back on, twice as wide and twice as bright as before. 'Quentin?' she said. 'Quentin, is that you?'

A large smile broke out on De Havilland's face. 'Penelope!' he said, rising from his chair. 'I thought I recognised your voice.' He took her hand and kissed it lightly. 'How long is it since we last met?'

'Six months,' she said quickly. 'At the golf club barbecue.'

'Of course, of course,' said De Havilland. He was all smiles now, and his words oozed honey. 'It's always such a delight to see you, my dear,' he continued. He stole a quick glance at Joe and frowned. 'It's just a shame it's under such unfortunate circumstances.'

Mrs Carter looked at her son and shook her head sadly. 'I know, I know,' she said. 'He's such a worry to me, Quentin. He runs completely wild. There's nothing I can do, and his father's no help.'

'There, there...' said De Havilland, patting her hand. 'I'm sure he'll turn out alright in the end. He's just fallen in with a bad crowd, that's all.' He turned his murderous gaze on Charlie, Lucy and Max.

At that moment the door opened again, and both Max's and Lucy's parents walked in, all four looking worried and frightened. Joy Green was a forceful lady with a temper as fierce as a tropical storm. As soon as she saw Max, she took two strides across the office and grabbed him by the scruff of his jacket.

'Ow, Mum! You're hurting!'

'Maximillian Green, what is the matter with you?' raged his mother as she wagged her finger in his face. 'Bringing shame like this on your family! What would your grandma say? Just wait until I get you home.' Poor Max looked thoroughly miserable, and he stared down at the floor.

Ken Yeung stood at the door with folded arms and frowned. He was a serious man, lean and fit from his years as an athletic coach. He glared at Lucy. 'So, this is what you get up to when we think you're at the gym?' Lucy couldn't bear to look at him.

Max's dad, Tony, was introducing himself to Mr

De Havilland. He was a mild-mannered man who liked to laugh, but tonight he looked like he carried the weight of the world on his shoulders. 'We're so sorry for the trouble our son has caused you, sir,' he said. 'If there is anything we can do to make amends, please tell us what it is.'

Max thought he would die of shame seeing his dad apologise to Mr De Havilland. More than anything he wanted to blurt out that the man was a criminal, but he couldn't. They could hardly start changing their stories now.

De Havilland nodded gravely to Mr Green and then turned to the police officer. 'So what will happen to these children now, officer?'

The officer folded her notebook. 'That all depends on whether or not you want to press charges, Mr De Havilland.'

De Havilland nodded again. 'Yes. Yes, I see,' he said. He glanced at the other parents and then sniffed. 'Well, I suppose there's not too much harm done. Thanks to the quick reactions of

Sharkey and myself, we were able to intervene before any serious crime was committed. As long as there is no repeat of this behaviour, I'm prepared to let the matter drop. Now if you'll all excuse me, I must be getting back to my boat. I'm sailing for France in the morning, and I shan't be back for at least a month. Good evening to you all.' And with that he raised his cap briefly to Mrs Carter and left.

Lucy's dad looked at his daughter and held the door open. He gave a quick jerk of his head. 'Go and get in the car, Lucy,' he said. 'We'll discuss your behaviour when we get home.'

'Come along, Maximillian,' said Max's dad. 'We also have some talking to do.'

'Wait a moment, please,' said Max suddenly. He turned to Charlie. 'What about you, Charlie?' he said. 'Your parents aren't here yet.'

Charlie said nothing, but she looked furious. Her lips were clamped tightly together, and she stared straight ahead, not looking at Max.

'We spoke to Miss Wells's mother over an hour

ago,' said the police officer. She glanced down at her notes. 'But she didn't seem too willing to come out.'

Charlie bit her lip. 'Mum doesn't like leaving the house after dark,' she said. 'I'll be okay to get home on my own.'

The officer sighed and pulled on her cap. 'I don't think so,' she said. 'Come on, I'll run you home myself. I think I'd like a chat with your mother.'

They started towards the door, but at the last moment Max darted forwards and pressed something into Charlie's hand. 'Here,' he said, 'this is for you. I found it in the dinghy. I know you'll know what to do with it. It's up to you now.' Then he turned and followed his parents out of the door, leaving Charlie and Sherlock alone with the police officer and Mr Creech.

Charlie stared after Max for a moment and then looked down at the thing Max had given her. Sitting in the palm of her hand was a feather. It was dark blue at the tip, yellow at the base, and multiple shades of green in the middle. It was like no feather she had ever seen before.

She stared at it for several seconds and then quietly put the feather in her pocket. And at that moment, she knew exactly what it was that Mr De Havilland and Sharkey were up to.

12

GROUP CHAT

Joe: Hello?

Joe: Hello?

Joe: Anyone there? Anyone at all?

Lucy: Hi.

Joe: At last. I've been messaging for two days now. No one answers.

Lucy: My folks took my phone away when they grounded me. I haven't been allowed to leave the house or talk to anyone all week.

Joe: What about your training?

Lucy: Dad borrowed a treadmill and put it in the garage. I have to look at a brick wall when I run now.

Joe: Grim.

Joe: So, apart from that, how did your folks take it?

Lucy: How do you think, Joe? They grounded me until after Christmas.

Joe: Bad luck. My mum took it pretty badly too. She kept going on about how much I'd embarrassed her in front of Mr De Havilland. Apparently, he's some sort of bigwig in the golf club, and now Mum thinks she's going to be a social outcast. She called up Dad just so he could shout at me over the phone, long distance. Then she took my phone away. Luckily I've got a spare she doesn't know about.

Lucy: My folks were furious too. At first, anyway. After that I think they were just in shock.

Joe: You shouldn't feel bad. Every kid gets themselves into trouble at some point. It happens to me all the time.

Lucy: I didn't get myself into trouble, Joe. You did. You got all of us into trouble.

Joe: Me? How?

Lucy: *'Of course I have permission to take out my parents' motorboat.'* – does that sound familiar?

Joe: Sorry. I just thought it would be fun. I didn't think it would end so badly.

Joe: You still there?

Lucy: Yes. I'm still mad at you though.

Joe: Did you hear from the others?

Lucy: How would I? Dad only gave me my phone back today. Max is probably in the same position. His parents are even stricter than mine. I don't know about Charlie though.

Max: Hey. Did I miss much?

Lucy: Max! How are you? Is everything okay at home?

Max: Well, the hurricane is over, but now the ice age has begun.

Lucy: ?

Max: At first Mum wouldn't stop yelling. I lost track of the things she threatened to do to me.

Now she's calmed down a bit, but she's stopped talking to me. She talks to my dad and to Saffy, but she pretends I'm not there. I think I preferred the yelling.

Joe: Don't worry, you just need to give her time to get over it.

Max: Thanks, but I need advice from you like I need a hole drilled in my skull.

Lucy: How long are you grounded?

Max: Until New Year.

Lucy: That's harsh.

Max: Yeah, but at least they're letting me use my computer. That's how I logged on to the group chat. Something strange has happened.

Lucy: Nothing could be stranger than the last three days.

Max: You remember that tracking device I planted on De Havilland's boat?

Lucy: How could I forget?

Max: Well, I thought the police would have found it. But when I checked, I discovered it was still sending out a signal, and I began to track it. The day after he caught us, De Havilland's boat sailed away from the coast and disappeared out of range.

Joe: So what? He said he was going to France and he wouldn't be back for a month.

Max: Yes, but now he's back.

Lucy: What? How?

Max: I don't know. The signal just appeared again the night before last. He's anchored a couple of miles offshore. Not moving at all.

Joe: Why would he do that?

Lucy: I bet he's come back to finish what he started.

Max: Exactly what I thought. He still needs to offload his merchandise, and he's waiting for the right time to do it.

Joe: Is he still there?

Max: That's just it. The signal has just begun moving again. He's moved closer to the shore. I think he's going to do it tonight.

Lucy: Well, there's nothing we can do now.

Joe: We can't even tell anyone. They wouldn't believe us.

Charlie: *$&** Im here*

Lucy: Charlie, good to hear from you. You locked down too?

Charlie: no my mum wdnt dre try it. Bt she ws hrrble 2 S.lock tho – it ws awfl…$.

Joe: Are you okay, Charlie? Your messages aren't making much sense.

Charlie: I cnt hlpit $ itsa chep phone & its dffcult 2 typ txts on it.

Lucy: Well, I'm just glad you're alright. Is Sherlock okay?

Charlie: Ys hes fne thk gdness. Listn – I ned to tell u smthnng. Is Mx ther?

Max: I'm here. Where else would I be?

Charlie: I chckd out tht feathr u gv me. The 1 u found on the boat.

Max: What about it?

Charlie: Its not frm hre, its v rarre. Then I figurd

it out. I kno what dehavlland is up to. we hv to stp him.

Lucy: Stop him doing what? We can't understand you, Charlie.

Lucy: Charlie? Are you still there?

Charlie: Sry – Rlly bad wifi hr. I cnt explain properly rt now. But I thnk de havvlland mght be cming bk sn.

Max: He is coming back soon. In fact, I think he's coming back tonight. I've been tracking his boat.

Joe: Charlie? Are you still there?

Charlie: Im thnkng#

Charlie: I thnk Dehavvland is goig to unlod his merch tonite. We hav to try & stp him.

Lucy: Stop him how, Charlie? We're all grounded in our bedrooms.

Charlie: Well u nd 2 get out smhw. I'll mt you by the sea wall wher we met the 1st nite.

Max: Charlie, we can't get out. What part of grounded don't you understand?

Charlie: I dnt care – ths is mor impt. Lives r at stake. I tht u wr my frnds?

Lucy: We are your friends, Charlie. But what do you mean, lives are at stake? Whose lives?

Charlie: Jst come & Ill xplain whn u get hr.

Max: Like we said, Charlie, we're all grounded. We can't get out.

Charlie: Fine. if u wnt help me ill go by mself. CU around.

Lucy: Charlie, don't do anything stupid. Those men are dangerous. You can't go on your own.

Max: Charlie, are you still there?

Joe: I think she's turned off her phone.

Lucy: I'm really worried. If those men are coming back, she might get herself into serious trouble.

Max: Well, what can we do? I wasn't lying about being locked in my room.

Joe: You should do what I do when I want to get out without being seen. I climb out of my bedroom window.

Max: Climb out the window? Have you seen how short my legs are?

Joe: I'm serious. I can climb out onto the swimming pool roof and get down from there.

Lucy: Not all of us have swimming pools, Joe.

Joe: I know. But my dad has a ladder round the back of the house. I could bring it over to your place, and you could use that. It will be fine. Trust me.

Max: I seem to remember you saying something like that that shortly before WE ALL GOT ARRESTED!

Joe: Look, I know I messed up before. And I understand if you and Lucy don't trust me. But Charlie is our friend, and I'm worried too.

Max: I hate to admit it, but you've got a point.

Joe: What about you, Lucy?

Joe: Lucy?

Lucy: I'm thinking.

Max: Well, don't think about it too long. I've just looked at my computer. De Havilland is on the move again. It looks like he's on the way to the sea wall where we saw the wrecker.

Lucy: Oh no! Charlie's out there by herself. Alright, let's do it. Joe, how quickly can you get over here?

Joe: Give me ten minutes. We'll be around for you straight after, Max.

Lucy: Please hurry. Charlie's all on her own – I'm really worried about her.

13

ESCAPE

Charlie ran through the deserted winter streets at the north end of town, cursing the cold weather, cursing the fact that she hadn't thought to bring a warmer jacket, and cursing the fact that she was on her own again. It had been nice to have friends, if only for a short while. But it always ended up the same way. Whenever you were beginning to trust someone, they always let you down.

She glanced down at the little dog running at her side. He looked up and *ruff*ed at her. Sherlock had no notion of where they were going, but he was just happy to be with the girl he loved more than anything in the world. 'If only all my friends were as loyal as you, Sherlock,' she said with a smile.

As she and Sherlock crossed the car park by the boating lake and approached the sea wall, they slowed to a walk. She could tell by the sound of the waves that the tide was out. She clambered up onto the concrete wall and looked out over the darkened sands to the granite rocks where Sherlock had fallen and so nearly drowned.

Her heart sank. When she had learned from Max that De Havilland's boat was on the move, she had been sure she would see the ghostly fisherman standing on the granite blocks, waving his lantern, just as they had seen him on the first night. But there was nothing to see apart from the waves crashing against the rocks. She had been wrong.

And then she saw it. Out at sea, a solitary light blinked once in the darkness. It was hard to tell how far away it might be. She climbed down off the wall and got out of sight in the deep shadows. The light blinked again, and again, and she realised that it was a small boat heading inland, right towards the spot where she was hiding.

She heard the faint sounds of an outboard motor and saw a dark shape pushing through the breakers as it headed towards the beach. There could be no mistake now. It was the same dinghy that Max had placed his tracking device in only a few nights ago, only now the boat appeared to be laden with boxes. De Havilland had returned to deliver his merchandise.

She watched carefully as the dinghy drew closer to the beach, and bit her lip. Should she run now to fetch the police so they could catch De Havilland red-handed? Or should she wait until her suspicions were confirmed and she saw them unloading the goods? And where was the ghostly fisherman they had seen signalling from the beach that first night? Something about this didn't feel right.

Sherlock barked once. 'Quiet,' she hissed.

Sherlock barked again, louder this time. 'I said

quiet!' She looked down at him and frowned. 'You'll give us away.'

'It's too late for that!'

Charlie gasped at the sound of the harsh voice close behind her. A big hand grabbed her by the shoulder and whirled her around roughly, and she found herself face to face with the mysterious fisherman. The man bared his teeth in a snarl and she could see straight away that he was not a ghost or a spectre. He was just a man.

'Let me go!' yelled Charlie. 'You've got no right to do this.' She tried to struggle, but the man was too strong for her.

Sherlock was barking madly at the fisherman now. The man glanced down and aimed a kick at the little dog, but Sherlock ducked out of the way and backed out of range of the man's boot. Keeping hold of Charlie with one hand, the man picked up a stone and hurled it in Sherlock's direction. It struck the dog on the rump, and he turned and fled into the darkness with a yelp.

'Sherlock!' screamed Charlie. She tried to kick out at the man, but he was too strong for her. He grabbed Charlie by the scruff of her jacket and lifted her so that her feet were very nearly off the ground. Then he marched her towards the beach, where the boat was just coming into land.

The tiny stone bounced off the glass with a barely audible *ping*. A moment later it was followed by another. Then another. Then a handful of stones clattered against the window like hail on a tin roof. 'Lucy! Are you up there?'

The window was thrown open, and Lucy's head stuck out. She was wearing a black tracksuit with her hair tucked up into a black beanie. 'Quit making so much noise down there,' she hissed.

Joe stepped out of the shadows and grinned up at her, pushing his hair out of his eyes. 'I've been trying to get your attention for ages.'

'My dad was in the next room,' she answered. 'I had to wait until he went downstairs. Did you bring the ladder?'

Joe reached into the shadows and proudly pulled out the stepladder he had brought with him, placing it on the ground beneath Lucy's window. It was about five steps high and barely reached the ground-floor windows, let alone Lucy's bedroom.

'Is that it? How am I meant to get down with that?'

Joe shrugged. 'Sorry,' he said. 'I thought it would reach further.'

Lucy rolled her eyes. 'Oh boy, you'd be useless in a prison break,' she said. 'My cat would be more help than you. Just get out of my way.'

She swung a leg over the windowsill. 'What are you doing?' asked Joe in alarm.

'Escaping from my bedroom without your help,' she replied.

Lucy held on to the window frame with one hand and reached along the wall for the iron drainpipe that ran down from the bathroom next to her bedroom. When she had curled her fingers around it, she placed the sole of her trainer on the wall and swung herself out of the window, grasping the drainpipe with both hands as she did. Joe watched with admiration as she climbed swiftly down the pipe, moving hand over hand like a squirrel.

She jumped the last metre and landed beside Joe, who was staring at her wide-eyed with admiration. 'Wow!' he said. 'I don't know anyone who can climb as well as you.'

'Thanks.' Lucy checked her watch. 'Okay, let's get moving. If my dad discovers I'm gone, I'll be grounded until I'm a little old lady.'

They picked up Joe's ladder and sprinted along the alley behind Lucy's house. At the main road, they headed down the hill towards the parade of shops where Max's parents had their computer repair shop.

In another alleyway behind the parade, they located Max's bedroom. 'Third one from the end,' said Lucy. 'The one with the *Warlocks and Dragons* stickers in the window.'

Joe frowned. '*Warlocks and Dragons*?'

Lucy rolled her eyes. 'What can I say? The boy's a hopeless geek.'

At that moment, the window to Max's bedroom went up, and he looked out, blinking in the semidarkness. 'Joe, Lucy, is that you?' he hissed. 'Can you get me down? Where's the ladder?'

'Don't get your hopes up,' said Lucy. 'Joe's ladder turned out to be a bit of a disappointment. Can you get onto the flat roof?'

Max's bedroom looked out onto the flat roof of the stockroom at the back of their shop. It was a short climb down from the window, but Max looked at the roof dubiously. 'My dad's in there doing some repairs,' he said. 'If I walk across it, he might hear me.'

Lucy and Joe looked at the illuminated window of the stockroom and wondered how loud Max's footsteps might be to someone inside. 'There's no other way,' said Lucy in a whisper. 'Just go as quietly as you can. I'll climb onto the rubbish bins and help you down from there.'

'Give me a minute.' Max disappeared inside his bedroom and then reappeared a moment later holding his shoes in his hands. Moving gingerly, he began to climb out of his bedroom window. It was not done as gracefully as Lucy's exit. Max put both legs over the edge of the windowsill and then turned onto his stomach and lowered himself down. There was a moment's pause while he had to unhitch his T-shirt, which had become caught in the window catch, and then he was standing on the flat roof with his shoes in his hand.

He hoisted his rucksack onto his shoulder and began to tiptoe across the flat roof. A sudden creak from the boards beneath his feet made him stop and hold his breath in terror. When it was clear that Max's dad wasn't coming out to investigate, he continued to the far side of the roof, where Lucy was already standing on the bins, waiting for him.

'Take my bag first,' he hissed, handing down the rucksack. 'It's got some things I might need.'

Lucy passed the bag down to Joe and then went back for Max. 'Lower yourself down from the roof with your arms,' she called up to him. 'Then drop. I'll catch you.'

Moving very carefully, Max lay face down on

the roof and began to edge backwards. First his legs came over the edge, then his stomach until finally he was hanging by his arms, his feet just above Lucy's head.

'Wait until I get into a better position,' said Lucy. 'Don't let go.'

'Did you say "let go"?' came Max's muffled voice. 'Okay then.'

A moment later the rounded figure of Max dropped from the roof and landed right on top of Lucy. The bins toppled beneath her feet, and the pair of them went sprawling in the shop's back yard. Empty tins and bottles spilled across the yard, and a large tomcat streaked out from the shadows, hissing loudly as it escaped.

'You call that catching?' groaned Max as he sat up amidst the rubbish.

'You call that jumping?' snapped Lucy. 'I told you to wait.'

They were interrupted by the sound of a key being turned in the back door. 'It's my dad!' said

Max in a near hysterical whisper. 'He's heard us. Run for it!'

Three shadows sprinted out of the yard and around the corner just as the door swung open and Tony Green stepped out. He stood for a moment, scanning the debris strewn across his yard. Then he placed his hands on his hips. 'Wretched cats,' he muttered and went back inside.

The three children ran until they reached the far end of the alleyway. 'Stop, stop!' gasped Max. 'Please stop.'

'Don't say you're out of breath already,' said Lucy. 'We've hardly gone fifty metres.'

'It's not that,' panted Max. 'It's my feet.'

'What's wrong with your feet?' asked Joe.

'I left my shoes behind,' groaned Max. 'On the roof. These stones are sharp.'

'Max!' said Joe. 'How could you be so stupid?'

'It's not my fault,' insisted Max. 'You guys were hurrying me, and I was worried about getting caught. I got flustered, that's all. What am I going to do? I can't run all the way down to North Parade in my socks. My feet will be in a terrible state.'

Joe stared at Max. 'Seriously? We're on the track of a ruthless gang of criminals, and you're worried about your *feet*?'

'Hang on,' said Lucy. 'We can use this.' At the entrance to the alley was a pile of black rubbish bags and an overturned shopping trolley. Lucy dragged the trolley off the heap and turned it over. 'Alright, get in.'

Max blinked. 'What?'

'In the trolley,' she said. 'We'll have to wheel you.'

Max saw there was no time to argue. With some effort he heaved himself into the wire basket and sat down, with his legs sticking out in front of him. Lucy and Joe took the handle and began to push the trolley along the street. The trolley squeaked like a box full of angry mice, and one of the wheels wobbled terribly, but at least they were moving.

'Are you guys okay?' said Max, in a shaky voice.

'We'll manage,' said Lucy as they leaned into the hill. 'But as soon as this thing is over, I'm taking you running. You have *got* to get in better shape.'

14

SHOWDOWN

The trolley trundled squeakily along the seafront, past the entrance to the old pier, heading towards the sea wall. Joe and Lucy were pushing while Max jiggled around inside. 'This-is-really-uncomfortable,' gasped Max. He was struggling to hold on to the trolley with one hand while he looked at his phone.

'Oh, yeah?' snapped Lucy. 'You really ought to try being on our end of things. Please tell me that we're nearly there.'

Max squinted at the phone screen as it jiggled in his hand. 'It's difficult to tell,' he said. 'The signal from the tracking device is getting really faint. I think the battery must be nearly dead.'

'There's something coming this way,' said Joe suddenly.

They stopped pushing and looked where Joe was pointing. Something small and white was running full tilt along the promenade towards them.

'It's Sherlock!' cried Lucy. 'Come here, boy.'

Sherlock ran to the three children, barking madly. He refused to allow any of them to pet him, but he ran around them in tight circles, making a huge noise. Then he ran back in the direction he had come from before returning and barking some more.

Max had clambered out of the shopping trolley and was watching the dog curiously. 'I think he's trying to tell us something,' he said. 'I think maybe he wants to take us to Charlie.'

'Oh no!' said Lucy. 'You don't think something's happened, do you?'

'I don't know,' said Max, tapping his phone. 'But

it looks like De Havilland's boat has just pulled up by the sea wall at exactly the same place we saw Joe's ghost for the first time. Come on, we can follow Sherlock, but let's go quietly.'

Joe took off his belt and looped it under Sherlock's collar to use as a lead. 'Come on, boy,' he said. 'Show us where to find Charlie.'

Sherlock did not need telling twice. He took off along the promenade, straining at the belt-leash and dragging Joe along behind him. Lucy followed them closely while Max, shoeless, hobbled along some distance behind.

At the end of the promenade, Sherlock led them through the empty car park to the stretch of barren concrete behind the sea wall. When Max arrived, puffing and panting, the three of them peered cautiously over the wall onto the beach below.

The tide was out quite a long way, and they could see a dark stretch of wet sand where a large rubber dinghy had been hauled up out of the water. 'That's it!' said Max, checking his screen again. 'It's definitely De Havilland's boat.'

Two men were unloading crates and stacking them on the sand while a third stood in the boat, handing out the boxes and casting suspicious looks towards the distant light of Southwold in case anyone approached from that direction. Lucy could not see any of them clearly in the darkness, but she felt certain that the man in the boat was De Havilland and that the other two were his accomplices, Sharkey and the man they had called Dean.

'Look, there's Charlie,' gasped Lucy. One of the two men had reached behind some rocks and pulled out a small struggling figure whose hands appeared to have been tied.

'Oh no!' said Joe. 'They've caught her.'

They watched Charlie, still struggling with the man, as she aimed a kick at his leg. Then they heard her voice shouting above the noise of the waves. 'Get your grubby hands off me!'

'It's Charlie, alright,' said Joe. 'What are we going to do?'

'I don't know,' said Lucy desperately. 'We're no match for those three men, but I don't think we have time to go for help.'

But there was someone who knew what to do. As soon as he saw Charlie struggling with one of the men, Sherlock leaped forwards, pulling the makeshift lead out of Joe's hands and bounding down the steps of the sea wall. Before Joe could stop him, he had leaped onto the sand and was running towards the three men, barking and snarling so loudly that he sounded like a whole pack of dogs.

The two men looked terrified as Sherlock charged at them. The little dog barked and snapped and ran around them in angry circles, yet managed to stay just out of their reach. But when he had forced the men to back up to the edge of the sea, Sherlock promptly turned and disappeared into the darkness again.

'It's that vicious dog I told you about!' yelled Dean. 'The same one as before. It's like some sort of hound from hell.'

'Where did he go?' yelled Sharkey. 'If that dog's here, then the rest of those kids won't be far away.'

'Over there, you idiots,' shouted De Havilland from the boat. 'They're standing beside the sea wall.' He pointed straight at Lucy, Max and Joe, who were now standing in clear view at the top of the steps. 'Get them!' he cried.

Sharkey and Dean started running towards the three children. 'Uh-oh,' said Joe. 'They've rumbled us. Let's get a move on.' The three of them turned and began to run, not daring to look back at the two men lumbering after them.

If Joe and Lucy had been on their own, they might have escaped easily. But Max was still wearing only his socks, and they had gone only a few metres when he cried out in pain. 'My foot!' he yelled. 'I've trodden on something sharp.'

He sat down with a bump and clutched his injured foot.

Lucy and Joe turned just in time to see the two men catch up with Max and hoist him onto his feet. As Dean held on tightly to the boy, Sharkey shook his fist and yelled after Joe and Lucy.

'That's two of your friends we've got now,' he shouted. 'If you want to see either of them again, you'd better get yourselves back here right now!'

'What are we going to do now?' Joe's voice was trembling.

'We don't have any choice,' said Lucy. 'We have to go back.'

They walked slowly towards the two men. Lucy's heart was hammering in her chest as though she had run a half marathon, but she did her best to keep a calm expression. It wouldn't do to let these men see they were afraid of them.

Joe held up his hands and tried to force a smile. 'We don't want any trouble,' he said. 'We were just out for an evening walk. If you let our friends go, we'll be on our way.'

Sharkey turned and spat on the pavement to show what he thought of that. 'Out for a walk? D'you think I'm stupid?' he growled. 'You're the same kids we found snooping around our yacht the other night. You were warned to keep away from us, and you didn't listen, so now we're going to have to do things the hard way. Come on.'

He grabbed Joe and Lucy by their jacket collars and propelled them along in front of him as they walked back to the beach. Poor Max hobbled along as best he could, but it was obvious that his foot was hurting him a lot. 'Are you okay, Max?' asked Lucy.

'No talking,' growled Sharkey. He prodded Lucy in the back. 'Save it for when you see Mr De Havilland. He's going to have plenty of questions for you.'

They descended the steps to the beach, where De Havilland was waiting by the dinghy. Charlie was sitting on the sand by some rocks, with her hands still tied in front of her. When she spotted Lucy, Max and Joe, her eyes grew wider and her jaw dropped. 'You came after all,' she said in amazement.

'Hi, Charlie,' said Joe as they approached. 'We thought you might need some help.'

'As you can see,' said Max, 'it's going really well so far.'

De Havilland scowled at the children. 'I might have known the rest of you would be around here somewhere,' he said. 'So you couldn't resist coming back to stick your noses into my business again, could you? What are you, some sort of after-school detective club?' He paused to laugh at his own joke.

'We're good enough detectives to know what you're up to,' said Charlie. 'And I know exactly what you've got in those boxes.'

Max, Lucy and Joe looked puzzled while the three men began exchanged uneasy glances. 'You're lying,' said De Havilland. 'You've got no idea what's going on here.'

'You're smuggling animals,' said Charlie defiantly. 'Species of rare and endangered birds, to be precise.'

The three men looked horror-struck. 'You're just guessing,' De Havilland said, his face as dark as a winter storm. 'You've got no evidence.'

'Max found a feather on board your dinghy,' said Charlie. 'It took me ages to identify it properly because it's not from a British bird. It's from a really rare South American parrot called a blue-throated macaw. They're nearly extinct in the wild, but people like you smuggle them into the country and sell them to collectors for high prices. I read all about it.' She nodded towards the boxes stacked up on the beach. 'If I'm right, then I reckon those boxes are probably full of wild birds, all crammed tightly together. It's a cruel and horrible thing to do, and lots of them die on the journey.'

When Charlie had finished speaking, everyone fell silent, and they were suddenly aware of the sounds of rustling and muffled squawking coming from the boxes. Joe, Max and Lucy stared at the crates, wondering how many creatures were crammed in there.

De Havilland's look of anger had gradually given way to one of surprise. He stroked his chin thoughtfully. 'You're a lot smarter than I gave you credit for,' he said. 'But you got one thing wrong. I don't just deal in rare birds. I import anything my customers want. Snakes, turtles, monkeys, I even brought in a baby tiger once. No one suspects a respectable businessman like me with his own private yacht. It's the perfect cover and *very* profitable.'

'Well, it looks like your game's up, De Havilland,' said Joe bravely. 'Now we know what you're up to, it's only a matter of time before the police catch you.'

De Havilland chuckled. It was the sort of laugh people make when they know something that you don't know. It made a chill run down Joe's spine.

'Oh dear,' he said. 'Perhaps you're not so bright after all.' He pointed to the boxes. 'I've got over a hundred rare birds and reptiles in those crates, and I have buyers waiting for all of them. Do you really think I'm going to let you go talking to the police?' He nodded to Dean and Sharkey. 'Tie them all up,' he growled. 'After we've unloaded the goods, we'll take them back to the yacht and deal with them later.'

Dean and Sharkey looked at each other nervously. 'Er, I'm not sure about that, boss,' said Sharkey. 'That's kidnapping, isn't it?'

De Havilland's face twisted into a furious scowl, and he bared his teeth in a snarl that made Dean and Sharkey recoil. 'You idiots,' he growled. 'We'll all go to prison for ten years if those kids tell the police what they know. Is that what you want?'

Dean and Sharkey both shook their heads.

'Good. As soon as we've finished unloading, we're sailing back across the Channel. We'll take the kids to Belgium and dump them there. By the time they get home and tell their stories to the police, we'll be long gone. Now, do as I say.'

Sharkey looked unhappy, but he didn't argue. He collected a length of rope from the boat and began to cut it into shorter lengths. Dean wrapped a piece of the rough nylon cord around Max's wrists and pulled it tight.

Sharkey tied Lucy's wrists in a similar fashion. She grimaced as he tightened the knot but refused to cry out. Over Sharkey's shoulder, she noticed Joe. While no one was watching him, he was reaching inside his backpack. He saw Lucy looking and gave her a wink.

Dean shoved Max down onto the sand next to Charlie. Max turned to her. 'Well done for working out what they were smuggling,' he said. 'That was a piece of genius.'

'Thanks,' said Charlie. 'But it was teamwork. I'd never have figured it out if you hadn't found that feather.' She gave him a smile. 'I'm sorry I got so angry with you all earlier. Thanks for coming to rescue me.'

'For all the good it did,' said Max. 'It looks like we're all going to end up in Belgium.'

Sharkey turned to Joe with a piece of rope in his hand. 'You next,' he growled.

Joe chose that moment to make his move. As Sharkey came towards him, the boy took a step backwards. 'Stay away,' he cried, 'or I'll use this.' He pulled something from his bag, a thick red tube about the length of his forearm, which he held up with both hands.

'The boy's got a distress flare,' yelled De Havilland.

'And I know how to use it too,' said Joe in a shaky voice.

As Joe's eyes flicked between the men, Sharkey took a step forward. 'Now, don't do anything stupid,' he said. He narrowed his eyes and made a sudden lunge at Joe.

Several things happened in quick succession. There was a loud *pop* as Joe jerked the string hanging from the bottom of the red tube, then a *whoosh* like the sound of a rocket on fireworks night and a thin trail of smoke spiralled up into the sky. Then a distant *bang*, and a red star burst like a dying sun over their heads, bathing the whole beach in blood-red light.

15

THE DIAMOND-
BACKED
BOONDOGGLER

De Havilland took three strides across the sand towards Joe, with fury in his eyes. Joe started to run but immediately tripped over one of the boxes lying in the sand. He tried to scramble away, and, for a moment, it looked as though De Havilland might hit him, but then Lucy cried out.

'Leave him alone,' she yelled. 'Pick on someone your own size.'

De Havilland glared at Lucy, but then seemed to collect himself. He stepped back from Joe and straightened his jacket.

'You two,' he barked at Dean and Sharkey, 'get that last one tied up before he creates any more havoc. Then watch these kids while I go back to the yacht to collect the rest of the boxes.'

'But what about that flare?' said Dean, pointing at the red star that was now descending slowly towards the beach. 'The police will see it.'

'Calm down, you idiot,' said De Havilland. 'It's only been a few weeks since fireworks night. If anyone does see it, they'll just think that it's some kids messing around. Nobody is going to come and investigate. Now wait here while I get the rest of the merchandise, and don't let these kids give you any more trouble.' He threw the children a venomous glare before dragging the dinghy back into the waves. A minute later he had started the outboard motor and was chugging away towards his yacht in the distance.

Sharkey finished tying Joe's hands, then dragged the boy across the sand to sit next to his friends. 'Joe!' said Lucy as Sharkey shoved him down. 'Are you okay?'

Joe looked dazed. His long blond hair was in disarray, and there was a trickle of blood coming from his lip. But he smiled faintly at Lucy and gave her a thumbs up with one of his tied hands. 'I hit my mouth when I fell over,' he said. 'It hurts like anything, but it will be worth it if the police saw the flare. Do you think they'll come?'

By this time the bright red flare had dropped into the sea and had been extinguished, returning the beach to darkness. There was no sign of anyone coming to investigate, let alone the police. Lucy had a sinking feeling that De Havilland had been right. If anyone had seen it, they had probably just thought it was kids messing around.

Dean was still watching De Havilland's dinghy heading back to the yacht. His face was pale, and he wore a worried expression. 'Now what are we going to do, Sharkey?' he asked.

'We do what he told us to do,' said Sharkey. 'I'll watch the kids while you go and get the van. And hurry up, I want to get these crates off our hands.' He kicked at the pile of boxes with the toe of his boot, and immediately the sounds of rustling and squawking increased. It was clear that they were all crammed full of living creatures.

'Don't do that,' cried Charlie. 'They're defenceless animals.'

Sharkey laughed. 'It's nothing compared to what Mr De Havilland's going to do to you lot when he gets back,' he said. 'You won't all be so lively after a couple of days in the bottom of his boat.'

A strange smile crept across Lucy's face. 'You don't seriously think he's coming back, do you?' she said. 'He knows the police are probably on their way here now. He's gone back to the yacht to make his escape, and he's left you two to take the blame.'

Dean's eyes grew wider and more scared-looking. 'You don't think that's true, do you, Sharkey?' he said.

Sharkey scowled. 'Don't be an idiot,' he said.

'She's just winding you up, that's all. Take no notice.'

Lucy fixed her gaze on Dean. 'Think about it, Dean,' she said. 'He's left you here with all the evidence. There's nothing to connect him to the crime now. He can just deny everything.'

'She's right, Sharkey,' said Dean desperately. 'He's left us with all these animals. If they catch us now, we won't be able to prove a thing.'

Max, Joe and Charlie exchanged glances. They could see how much Lucy was unsettling Dean.

'Shut up!' snapped Sharkey. He loomed threateningly over Lucy, but Charlie picked up where Lucy had left off.

'You know she's telling the truth, don't you, Dean,' she said. 'Better run now while you've got the chance. It'll be ten years in jail for you both if you don't.'

'I warned you both,' snarled Sharkey. He strode across the sand and grabbed the collar of Charlie's jacket.

Charlie put up her tied hands to fend him off. But at that moment, something flew out of the darkness behind her. It was something small, with sharp teeth and a huge heart. It was Sherlock.

After Sherlock had run away, he had not gone far. As soon as he was out of sight, he had circled around the group on the beach and lay in wait, watching for his chance to save his beloved Charlie and her friends.

While the men were talking, he had crept back towards them. He'd approached under the cover of the rocks until he was no more than a few metres from where the children were sitting. But when he saw Sharkey grabbing hold of Charlie, he could stay quiet no longer.

The little dog leaped from the shadows, his ears flat and his teeth bared. Sharkey shrieked in panic, stumbling backwards into Dean before both men fell over the stack of boxes on the sand.

There was a crunch of breaking wood and a cacophony of screeching and shrieking from the animals inside. Several packages rolled onto the sand, and Max gasped. What he was looking at were parrots, tightly bandaged so that they could not move their wings. When he looked closer, he was shocked to see that some of them had their beaks taped together to prevent them making a noise. There were at least a hundred of the birds crammed into the narrow box.

Dean sat in the centre of a broken wooden box and was screaming at the top of his voice. 'The snakes!' he shrieked. 'The snakes are loose.' All around him was something that looked like a nest of tentacles, writhing and twisting and crawling all over him as he tried frantically to get away. 'Help me, Sharkey!' he wailed.

Sharkey swore under his breath, trying to catch sight of Sherlock, but the little dog had disappeared back into the darkness. 'When I catch that rat,' he growled, 'I'll wring its little neck.'

'Sherlock's too brave and too smart for you to ever catch him,' said Charlie. 'As long as you keep holding us here, he's never going to leave you alone.'

Sharkey looked like he might argue, but Dean's pleas were becoming frantic. 'Sharkey, please help me!' he cried. 'I'm terrified of snakes.'

Sharkey swore again and then went to help his companion. With his good hand he pulled Dean from the wreckage of the crate. Snakes of all sizes wriggled and squirmed to get away from the broken box.

As Dean was being pulled to his feet, he let out a hideous shriek of pain. 'It bit me!' he wailed.

He pointed a shaking finger at a particularly fat serpent that was slithering away across the wet sand. 'That one bit me!' he cried again. 'What's going to happen to me now?'

Max watched the large snake crawling away,

and an idea began to form in his brain. 'That's bad news, that is,' he said, adopting a fearful expression. 'That's a diamond-backed boondoggler.'

Dean looked as though he might faint on the spot. 'A d-diamond-backed b-b-boondoggler?' he said weakly. 'Are they p-poisonous?'

'Absolutely lethal,' said Max with a serious expression on his face. 'A single bite from a boondoggler can kill a grown man in less than half an hour.'

'Half an hour!' shrieked Dean. He turned in desperation to his accomplice and grabbed hold of his lapels. 'Help me, Sharkey,' he pleaded. 'I've been bit by a boondoggler. Get me to a doctor. I'm too young to die!'

Sharkey angrily shook himself free of Dean's grip. 'You're not going to die, you idiot,' he snapped. 'De Havilland said there were no poisonous snakes in this cargo. You've got nothing to worry about.'

'That's easy for him to say,' said Max. 'He's not the one who's been bitten by a boondoggler.

You'd better get medical attention right away before your blood starts turning to tar.'

'To t-tar?' repeated Dean.

'Tell me,' said Max, beginning to enjoy himself. 'Is your heart racing?'

Dean thought for a moment. 'Y-yes,' he said. 'It's thumping like a steam engine.'

'And are you feeling sweaty?'

Dean felt his brow. 'Yes,' he wailed. 'I'm sweating buckets here.'

Max sucked his teeth. 'That's bad, Dean,' he said. 'That's really bad.'

'Shut up, you,' snapped Sharkey. 'Dean, calm down. He's just trying to frighten you. Trust me, that snake wasn't poisonous.'

'You can't know that for sure,' wailed Dean. He began to back away from Sharkey. 'My blood might be turning to tar at this very minute. I've got to get to the hospital right away.' He staggered backwards along the beach.

'Dean, calm down!' yelled Sharkey. 'Nothing

bad is going to happen to you. And we've still got a job to do.'

Dean's breath was coming in hot gasps. 'I've-got-to-get to a hospital,' he said weakly. Clutching his bitten hand, he turned and ran away into the night.

'Dean, come back here!' yelled Sharkey. 'We need your van to load the boxes.' He swore again and began to chase after Dean.

The children watched the two men running away down the beach. 'Right!' said Max, scrambling to his feet. 'Everyone, start running.'

16

RESCUED!

The others did not need telling twice. Moving as quickly as they could manage with their hands tied, they scrambled to their feet and began to run in the opposite direction to the two men, heading towards the lights of the town.

'A diamond-backed boondoggler?' said Charlie as she jogged along the sand beside Max. 'There's no such thing. It was a baby python. They're completely harmless.'

'I know that, and you know that,' said Max. 'But Dean doesn't. Do you think he's still running?'

At that moment a small energetic shape bounded out of the darkness towards them.

Charlie fell to her knees in the sand. 'Sherlock!' she cried. 'My brave, brave boy. You saved all of us back there.'

'He's a real hero,' said Lucy, kneeling down beside Charlie. 'I don't think Sharkey or Dean knew what hit them.'

Max and Joe quickly helped each other to unpick the knotted ropes around their wrists. The men had been in a hurry, and fortunately the ropes were not difficult to undo. When they were free, they untied Lucy and Charlie, and then everyone joined in making a huge fuss of Sherlock.

The little dog had no idea what they were saying, but he knew that they were all very pleased with him, and that made him happy. As much as he loved Charlie, he had also missed her new friends over the last few days. He jumped around excitedly between the children, licking faces and rolling over in the sand to let his belly be tickled.

'We'd better get moving again,' said Lucy, glancing over her shoulder. 'They could be back any minute. Are you okay, Joe?'

Joe dabbed at the small cut on his lip and he grinned. 'It stings a bit,' he said. 'But I'll be fine.'

'I'm not sure I will be, though,' said Max. He had peeled off his sock and was examining his injured foot, which was cut quite badly. 'I think I might have a piece of glass in it.'

'We'll help you,' said Lucy. 'You can lean on me and Joe.'

Lucy and Joe helped Max to get up and placed his arms around their shoulders. Now that the initial excitement had worn off, Max's foot was really quite painful, and he had to hobble along slowly, supported by the others.

'Oh no!' said Charlie after they had gone a few steps. 'They're coming back.'

A hundred metres away, Sharkey was running up the beach towards them, closely followed by Dean. Dean had clearly got over his fear of being bitten by a boondoggler, and both men looked extremely angry.

'What are we going to do?' said Joe. 'Max can't run with his bad foot.'

'Go on without me,' said Max quickly. 'There's no sense in all of us getting caught.'

'No,' said Lucy quickly. 'We're friends, aren't we? That means we all stand together, and we don't leave anyone behind.'

Charlie and Joe nodded quickly, and Sherlock barked. 'That settles it,' said Lucy. 'We'll make these two wish they'd never tangled with us.'

They turned in a line to face the two men. Lucy, Joe and Max stood with clenched fists and grim expressions while Charlie held on to Sherlock's collar as they waited for the men to catch up with them.

When they were just a few paces away, the two men slowed to a walk. Sharkey scowled and bared his teeth. 'You've done it now,' he snarled. 'Half of Mr De Havilland's snakes have escaped, and it's all your fault. He's going to be *very* unhappy when he sees you.'

'Don't get any closer,' yelled Charlie. 'Not unless you want me to set my dog on you again.'

Sharkey sneered. 'That little rat?' he said. 'He might have a loud bark, but he's no match for this.' He reached behind his back and pulled something long and heavy from the waistband of his trousers. Max recognised it as an iron crowbar, of the sort used for opening crates. 'Let's see how brave he is after I hit him over the head with this.'

Charlie pulled Sherlock closer protectively. 'We're not afraid of you,' she said. But they all knew it was a lie.

The two men were both grinning now as they approached. 'You've caused us a whole heap of trouble,' said Dean. 'And now we're going to make you pay for it.'

Max felt as though someone had filled his belly with ice water, his legs were shaking, and his mouth had turned completely dry. It had been his idea to try to catch these smugglers, he told himself. And now his friends were going to get hurt because of it.

He was still thinking this when the beach was filled with a blinding white light. For a moment, Max thought it was another flare. Then wide torch beams began sweeping across the sand from somewhere behind them. There was shouting and the sounds of several people running towards them. Somewhere overhead, they could hear the noise of a helicopter.

Max looked at his friends, but it was obvious that they were as surprised as he was. A few metres away, Sharkey and Dean were wearing startled expressions as they shielded their eyes against the torch beams. Four officers in blue uniforms ran straight past the children towards the two men.

'It's the cops, Sharkey!' cried Dean. 'Run for it!'

The two men turned to flee, but were tackled to the ground by the police officers. Then the whole beach seemed to be filled with police. Two of them held on to Sharkey and Dean while another attached the handcuffs; others barked into radios or took notes in black notebooks. And nobody seemed to be paying attention to the children at all.

'What *is* going on?' asked Joe. He looked around at the others, but no one had any answers.

'Ah, so there you all are,' said a deep voice behind them.

They turned around to find themselves looking at a familiar figure, swinging a walking stick. The man had white whiskers and was wearing a naval cap and a pea-jacket.

'Captain Tom!' chorused the children together.

'That's me,' said the captain, touching the peak of his cap. He glanced over at the two men lying face down on the sand. 'I must say this looks like a nasty business,' he said. 'I'm very glad to find you all in one piece.'

'Captain Tom, what are you doing here?' said Lucy. 'And where did all the police come from?'

Captain Tom paused to lean on his cane. 'I was up in the lighthouse, doing my rounds as caretaker, when I spotted a group of children through my binoculars, heading towards the sea wall.' His eyebrows knitted together in a thick hedge. 'I wondered if it might be you lot after our conversation the other day. Then, a little while later, when I saw a flare go up from the beach, I began to get worried.'

'We didn't think anyone had seen it,' said Joe.

'I doubt that anyone did, apart from me,' said Captain Tom. 'Fortunately, I thought to call the police.' He looked around. 'As you can see, they came in force.'

Suddenly, everyone wanted to ask questions at once.

'Why are there so many of them?' said Lucy.

'Do they know about the smugglers?' said Joe.

'Has anyone told them there are animals over there that need help?' said Charlie.

'Did they catch Mr De Havilland?' said Max.

Captain Tom held up his hands for silence. 'Hold on, hold on,' he said. 'All in good time. I'm sure the police will want to talk to all of you, and there'll be plenty of time for questions. In the meantime' – he paused and glanced at Joe's split lip and Max's injured foot – 'it looks like you lot have been in the wars. Let's start by getting you all somewhere warm and dry.'

It turned out that Captain Tom's cottage was right on the seafront, close to the pier and near to where they were standing. Captain Tom spoke to one of the police officers, who appeared to be in charge, and then escorted the children across the road to his house.

Captain Tom's wife was a round and jolly woman named Vera, who was completely unfazed by her husband arriving home with four children and a dog, and she fussed around them as she welcomed them inside.

'Come in, come in, my dears,' she said, helping

Lucy out of her jacket. 'You're all soaked through and freezing cold too, I shouldn't wonder. And what on earth is going on with all the police out there? Smugglers, you say? Whatever next?'

Half an hour later they were sitting in Vera and Tom's front room, warming themselves by the fire while they sipped sugary tea and ate Vera's home-made scones with Captain Tom's special damson jam. Joe sported a huge lump on his lip, which he wore like a badge of honour as he explained for the third time to Captain Tom how he had escaped from the clutches of Mr De Havilland. Max sat with his injured foot in a bowl of warm water, to which Vera had added a cloudy splash of disinfectant, and Sherlock was crunching digestive biscuits on the hearth while Charlie sat beside him and stroked him fondly.

They were interrupted by a knock at the door, and two people entered. The first was the same uniformed police officer who had given them a telling-off in the Harbour Master's office a few nights ago. 'Not you lot again!' she said when she saw them. 'I might have known you'd be at the bottom of all this. Didn't you learn your lesson last time?'

The children looked guiltily at one another and then at the officer. Surely they weren't going to get into trouble again? Not after all they had been through this evening.

Lucy stood up. 'We're sorry if we caused you any trouble,' she said. 'But we were sure those men were up to no good. We were just trying to find some evidence to prove it.'

The officer frowned at the children. 'I see,' she said. Then, quite suddenly, she broke into a smile. 'Well in that case, I think you'd better have a word with the inspector here.'

She gestured to the tall man standing behind her in a raincoat. He had a kind face but with steel-grey eyes that seemed to miss nothing. 'My name is Inspector Callahan,' he said. 'And I'm very interested to meet the children who caught the notorious Jungle Crew.'

'The Jungle Crew?' said Max. 'What's that?'

The inspector accepted a cup of tea from Vera and nodded his thanks. There was a brief pause while he sipped and made appreciative noises. 'That was the name we gave to De Havilland and his gang,' he said. 'Some time ago, the police in London gave us a tip-off that they'd found a lot of rare creatures being sold illegally as pets. We suspected that there was a smuggling gang operating somewhere along this coast, but they always seemed to be one step ahead of us. Now we've caught them, thanks to you.'

'But what about Mr De Havilland?' asked Max. 'He went back to his yacht before you arrived. You have to hurry, or he'll get away.'

The inspector put down his cup and smiled as he accepted a scone with jam from Vera. 'Oh, don't worry about him,' he said. 'The coastguard caught him trying to escape across the Channel. They found all sorts of wild animals on board his boat. It turns out he's wanted in five different countries for smuggling endangered creatures.'

'What's going to happen to all those poor animals?' asked Charlie. 'Are they going to be alright?'

The inspector nodded gravely. 'Smuggling animals is a horrible business,' he said. 'And it's not unusual for many to die on the journey. But, thanks to you, they'll be fine. My officers have rounded most of them up safely, and they'll be cared for at a rescue centre until they can be returned to the wild again.' He put down his plate and dabbed his mouth with a napkin. 'What I don't understand,' he said, 'is what made you all suspect De Havilland? From what I hear, he's a very well-respected man in these parts.'

'It started when we saw the Spectre on the beach,' said Joe.

'And then Sherlock tore his trousers,' said Charlie.

'But afterwards we saw him talking to

Sharkey,' said Lucy.

'And then we took the motorboat and overheard Sharkey talking to Mr De Havilland on his yacht,' said Joe.

'Right before we planted the tracking device,' said Max.

The expression on the inspector's face became increasingly bewildered as the children were talking, until he held up his hands for silence. 'Whoa, whoa, wait just a minute,' he said. 'Spectre? Motorboat? *Tracking device?*' He put down the napkin and took out a notebook and pencil from his inside pocket. 'Perhaps you had all better start from the beginning.' He glanced over at the officer. 'And perhaps we should call their parents to come and collect them when we've finished?'

The children let out a collective groan. 'Not our parents,' said Max. 'My mum will go into orbit when she finds out I climbed out of my bedroom window.'

'And I'll be running on that treadmill for the rest

of my life,' said Lucy.

'My mum's going to be furious that we got Mr De Havilland arrested,' said Joe. Then he grinned. 'She'll never get invited to the golf club now.'

The inspector smiled as he took a seat in one of the armchairs. 'Well, I wouldn't worry too much about any of that,' he said kindly. 'From what I hear, you lot have been real heroes tonight. When your parents learn the true story, I think it's all going to turn out fine.'

17

FRIENDS

Max hurried along North Parade, pulling his duffel coat tightly around him. The bitter wind stung his cheeks, and the frozen puddles crackled beneath his feet as he walked. His mum said he must be mad going out on a night like this, but she had still let him go. She seemed to trust him a lot more these days.

The sudden snap of cold weather had kept most people inside on Christmas Eve, and Max was alone as he passed gardens filled with large, illuminated reindeers, inflatable snowmen, and fairy lights that blinked on and off to the tune of 'Jingle Bells'. But he smiled when he saw a tall and familiar figure walking along the street ahead of him.

'Hey, Luce!' he shouted. 'Wait up.'

Lucy stopped and turned as Max caught up. When he saw her up close, Max blinked in amazement. Underneath her overcoat, Lucy was wearing a red dress with a matching scarf, mittens and pumps. Her long black hair was untied from its usual ponytail, and it hung loosely around her shoulders.

'Wow,' he said. 'You look amazing. I don't think I've ever seen you not wearing a tracksuit.'

Lucy smiled. 'Why, thank you,' she said. 'And look at you! This is very nice.' She leaned forward and straightened his new bow tie, which was blue with large white spots on it.

'Thanks,' he said, pleased. 'It's not on elastic either. You really have to tie it properly. It was an early Christmas present from Mum. She said I'd better look smart if I was going to be in the papers.'

They descended the steps leading down to the

beach. 'So, what do you think this is all about?' asked Lucy as they crossed the soft sand. 'All I got was a message from Joe that said, *Be at the beach hut, 7 p.m., Christmas Eve. Wear something posh.*'

'Same here,' said Max. 'He wouldn't tell me anything else. But if Joe's planning something, we might all end up in jail by the end of the evening.'

They passed the neat rows of colourful beach huts, now shuttered and closed for the winter, until they reached the last hut on the row. There was no sign of anyone about.

'Where's Joe?' asked Lucy. 'You don't think he's stood us up, do you?'

'I wouldn't put it past him,' said Max. 'Try the door.'

Lucy mounted the steps and tried the door handle. She found it opened easily.

'Ladies first,' said Max.

Lucy stepped inside cautiously, closely followed by Max. It was pitch dark inside, but the air was warm.

'There's no one in here,' hissed Max. 'I told you.'

There was a soft *click*, and the inside of the little beach hut was suddenly transformed. A string of fairy lights in pink and blue lit up the tiny room and revealed Joe's grinning face, standing by the light switch. 'Surprise!' he yelled. He threw another switch, and a tiny Christmas tree in the corner suddenly burst into life with twinkling white lights.

Lucy clapped her hands. 'Oh, Joe!' she cried. 'It's beautiful in here.'

'It's fantastic,' said Max, peeling off his coat and taking a seat close to the fire. 'I feel like I could spend the whole of Christmas in here.'

Joe beamed with delight at the faces of his two friends. He hopped around the tiny space, lighting the oil lamp and putting the kettle on the little gas stove. 'I've barely seen any of you since the night the police arrested the smugglers, and I really wanted to get us all together,' he said. 'And then I remembered that Charlie said she and her mum never celebrated Christmas at home, so I thought we could do something special for her here.'

'That's such a lovely thought,' said Lucy. She looked around. 'So where is Charlie?'

Joe's face fell. 'I don't know,' he said. 'I sent her a message, but she never replied. Her phone's so old I don't know whether she got it or not, and I don't even know where her house is.' He looked at his watch. 'But I guess she's not coming now.'

They all fell quiet, feeling the absence of Charlie and Sherlock. 'So, anyway,' said Joe, breaking the silence, 'how did your folks all take it when they got another call from the police?'

'At first I thought my mum was going to go nuclear,' said Max. 'At one point she even threatened to send me to stay with my cousins to get me away from "bad influences".'

'Bad influences?' said Joe.

'She meant you lot,' said Max. 'But then Inspector Callahan explained how heroic we'd all been capturing the smugglers and how we're a credit to our families, and she changed completely.' He slapped his stomach happily. 'She's been giving me extra-large portions all week and telling Saffy that she should take an example from me. It couldn't have worked out better, really.'

'Same here,' said Lucy. 'Dad hit the roof when he first found out. But he calmed down when the inspector spoke to him. Then when the reporters came to our house, they photographed us together, and they described him as an "Olympic running coach". I think he was more pleased about that than anything else.'

'My mum was furious at first too,' said Joe. 'She kept going on about "poor Mr De Havilland", and she said that I'd made her a social outcast. She even made Dad come home early from his business trip specially so he could tell me off.'

'So, what happened?' asked Lucy.

'Well, by the time Dad got home, it was all over the papers,' said Joe. 'Then all of Mum's set began calling her to hear the story first-hand. She and Dad got invited to the Jackson-Foleys' for mulled wine and mince pies tonight. Mum was over the moon. She's been trying to get an invitation there for ages. Apparently, they're related to royalty.' He stuck his nose into the air and made them all laugh by pretending to drink tea with his little finger stuck out straight.

'I could get used to being famous,' said Max, reclining on the cushions. 'Toby Watts and his mates don't dare to touch me now. I walked past them at the bus stop on my way here, and they didn't say a word to me.'

'And did you see the papers?' said Joe. He reached into a large bag and slapped a thick wodge of newspaper down onto the table. There were several local papers and even a national edition that all carried a version of the same story about how the children had helped to catch De Havilland and his gang. '"Hero children outwit Jungle Crew",' said Joe, reading from a paper on the top of the pile.

'This one says the police have recommended us for a bravery award,' said Lucy. She looked down at her dress. 'I'm not sure where I'd pin it though.'

'There's a photo of all of us in this one,' said Max. 'But it makes me look really short.'

'I hate to break it to you, Max,' said Joe, 'but that's not an optical illusion.' He opened another paper to a centre-page spread, complete with diagrams of the beach and a picture of De Havilland's yacht. 'This one's got a story about how you built the tracking device, Max,' he said. 'It calls you a "child genius".'

Max made a show of breathing on his fingernails and then rubbing them on his lapel.

Lucy was reading a longer article in one of the local papers. Her jaw had dropped open, and her eyes opened wide. 'Did you see this?' she squeaked. 'It's an interview with Creech, the Harbour Master. He says he'd been suspicious of De Havilland all along and that he was the one who called the police and rescued us on the beach.'

'The dirty liar!' exclaimed Joe. 'Still, it's just like him to want to get in on the act.' He peered over Lucy's shoulder to look at the article. 'At least they included all our names,' he said. 'But I don't think Charlie will like it. They've called her "Charlotte".'

Lucy put down her paper and sighed. 'It's such a shame Charlie didn't come,' she said. 'It doesn't seem right to be here enjoying ourselves when she's not here. We'd never have solved the mystery if it hadn't been for her and Sherlock.'

The others nodded and fell silent again. Then Joe brightened. 'Hey, is anyone hungry?' He reached into the bag again and produced a large frying pan. 'I thought we could have fried eggs and sausages. I'd even brought some vegetarian sausages for Charlie.'

Max and Lucy laughed. 'Good grief, Joe,' said Lucy. 'How much more stuff have you got in that bag?'

Max squinted into the bag and pulled out a packet of sausages and a box of eggs. 'Well,' he said slowly, 'I had three helpings of dinner earlier.' Then he grinned. 'But that was nearly an hour ago, so, yeah, I could eat sausage and eggs.'

Joe jumped up and put the pan on the cooker and started heating the oil. When the kettle boiled, he made more of his special lumpy hot chocolate and passed the mugs around. As he was placing

Max's mug down on the table, there was the tiniest of scratches at the door. Then it swung open to reveal Charlie and Sherlock standing in the entrance.

Charlie gave them a small smile. 'Is it okay?' she said. 'If we come in, I mean? We're not interrupting anything, are we?'

The others stared at her in amazement for a moment, and then Joe cried out, 'Charlie! Sherlock! Of course you're not interrupting anything. I organised this *for you!* So that you could have a real Christmas.'

He bounded towards Charlie and gave her a huge hug, lifting her off her feet in the process. Sherlock barked and leaped up onto the benches, where he proceeded to lick Max and Lucy's faces as though they were covered in ice cream and he, Sherlock, had been given the very important task of getting it all off.

Charlie looked startled as Joe spun her around. When he put her down, she was pink and breathless. 'Wow,' she said, looking around at the Christmas tree and the lights. 'Do you really mean it? You did all of this for me and Sherlock?'

'It was Joe's idea,' said Lucy. 'Isn't it great?'

Charlie beamed and took a seat between Max and Lucy while Joe made her some hot chocolate. Then he started to fry up the sausage and eggs, filling the cabin with delicious hot smells.

'This is so brilliant,' said Max as Joe placed four plates of food on the table and another, smaller plate with two sausages on the floor for Sherlock. 'I'm half starved.'

'I still can't believe you did all this for me and Sherlock,' said Charlie, who had not been able to stop staring at the Christmas tree. 'I thought... I thought after it was all over and we'd solved the mystery that you wouldn't want us around any more.'

'Why on earth wouldn't we want you around?' said Joe.

Charlie shrugged. 'I don't know. Whenever I

meet new people, I usually end up being rude to them or getting angry so that they start hating me. I guess I just never managed to stay friends with anyone this long before.' She turned and smiled at each of them in turn.

'Of course we're still friends,' said Lucy.

'And heroes,' said Joe.

'Don't forget "child geniuses",' added Max.

'We're all of those things,' said Lucy.

'I'll drink to that,' said Joe, raising his mug.

They clinked their mugs of lumpy hot chocolate and laughed, recalling their adventures of the last few days. It turned out that Joe had also brought a large carrot cake from the kitchen cupboard at home, which he cut up into five hefty chunks and which Max and Sherlock managed to eat most of. Then Joe had one last surprise.

From the very bottom of his bag he produced four presents wrapped in an untidy, rumpled way. There was a new water bottle for Lucy that she could take on her runs and a stylish new tie for

Max. Charlie had a guidebook of British birds, and Sherlock had a rawhide bone. He woofed delightedly when Charlie unwrapped it for him and set to chewing it on the rug.

'This has been the best Christmas ever,' said Charlie as she hugged her knees in delight. 'Thanks so much for being my friends.'

'So, can we call ourselves a gang now?' said Joe.

'Or how about a crew?' said Max.

'What was it that De Havilland called us?' said Lucy. 'Oh, I remember. He said we were like an "after-school detective club". That's what we should call ourselves.'

They all agreed that was an excellent name and sealed it with more hot chocolate and carrot cake until they could barely move. 'Oh gosh, is that the time!' said Lucy. 'I promised I wouldn't be late. There's still loads of wrapping to do at home.'

'Me too,' said Max, standing up and stretching.

They packed away the dirty crockery and the

remains of the food into Joe's bag and then turned off the Christmas tree lights and filed outside.

'Hey, look at that,' said Lucy, staring upwards.

The others followed her gaze and saw that thick white flakes of snow were floating down gracefully and settling on the sand. The beach was beginning to turn white.

'It really *is* a white Christmas,' said Joe.

'Let's all promise to meet up in the new year,' said Charlie.

'I'll second that,' said Lucy.

'Sure,' said Max, patting his belly again. 'But let's get Christmas out of the way first, shall we? I have a *lot* of eating to do before then.' And they all laughed as they walked arm in arm along the beach in the direction of home.

The After-School Detective Club are back in

The Secret of Ragnar's Gold.

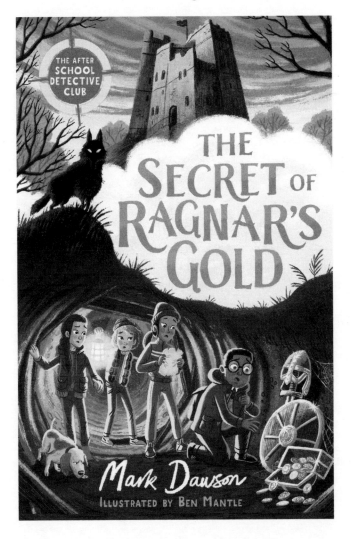

Read on for a preview of the opening chapter . . .

1

PLOTS AND PLANS

Joe's parents were arguing.

This was not unusual. Joe's father travelled on business for a large part of the year and Joe missed him terribly. But whenever he was home, his mum and dad would start arguments that sometimes lasted right up until the point when his dad left on business again.

Today's argument was about the surprise holiday his dad had arranged. Joe sat at the kitchen table with his head down, pretending to do his homework, but he was listening carefully as his dad explained the plan.

'I've already told you, Penny,' said his dad. 'It's a castle. A *real* castle. One of my clients bought it as an investment and he's part way through renovating it. He says we can use it and he's given me the keys. It's got battlements and big fireplaces and even a moat.' He moved closer to his wife and slipped an arm around her shoulder. 'Come on, it'll just be the three of us. Imagine what a wonderful time we'll have.'

Joe was already imagining what sort of fun he could have in a castle. He pictured himself in a large banqueting hall, throwing leftover bones to the dogs, or standing guard on the drawbridge with a sword in his hand. He wondered if the castle had suits of armour and swords and stuff like that. If it did, he was sure nobody would mind too much if he borrowed one for a bit of sword practice.

Unfortunately, Penelope Carter was not a castle sort of person. She did not much care for history, or places that were cold or damp, nor did she much enjoy spending time with 'just the three of them'. What Penelope Carter did like was sunshine and beaches and cocktails and glamorous people with impossibly deep suntans who wore designer clothes. She greeted her husband's plans with folded arms and a face like stone.

'Well, this is *typical* of you, Mike,' she said. 'You arrive home with some half-baked plan about going to a castle that you imagine we'll think is wonderful.'

As it happened, Joe did think the plan sounded pretty wonderful but he knew that now was probably not the best time to say so.

'Did you stop to think about whether it was something *I* might want to do?' she asked. 'Did you even bother to ask if *I* had anything planned for the holiday?'

Mike Carter stared blankly at his wife. 'Well, do you have anything planned for the holiday?'

'As a matter of fact, yes,' said Penelope. 'Maria Santorini called while you were away and invited us to spend the week on their yacht in the Mediterranean. Apparently, everyone who's anyone in fashion will be there. I accepted, of course.'

Joe groaned inwardly at the thought of a week spent on a yacht with people he didn't know who talked about fashion the entire time.

His father wasn't quite ready to give up just yet. 'But, Penny,' he pleaded. 'Couldn't we just—'

'No, we could not,' said Penelope Carter firmly. 'You seem to forget that I had a career in fashion once, Mike. And if you think for one minute that I am going to miss the chance of catching up with my old friends to go and stay in a draughty old *castle*' – she spat out the word as though it tasted bad – 'then you don't know me very well.'

Mike Carter's shoulders drooped in defeat and Joe could see the castle holiday slipping away. He decided that now was the time to intervene. 'But, Mum,' he pleaded, 'staying in a castle would be brilliant. And it's totally educational. Besides, I really don't want to spend a week on a yacht.'

'Well, that's very fortunate, Joseph,' said his mother. 'Because you are not invited.'

Joe frowned. 'What?'

'That's right, it's adults only, I'm afraid,' said his mother. Joe's mouth dropped open. 'Now don't pout, darling. You said yourself you wouldn't enjoy it for one minute. I called your grandmother and I've arranged for her to come and look after you for the week. I'm sure you'll both have a lovely time.'

'But Mum—' began Joe.

Penelope Carter held up a solitary finger. 'Sorry, but I'm not going to hear another word on the subject of castles. Your father and I are going to stay on a yacht, and you, Joe, are staying here with your grandmother and that's all there is to it. Now, if you'll excuse me, I'm going to pack.'

Before either of them could say another word, Penelope swished out of the room, leaving Joe and his father to stare at each other helplessly.

'Sorry, Joe,' said his dad. 'I thought the castle would be a good idea.'

'It *is* a good idea, Dad,' said Joe. 'Couldn't you persuade her to—'

'I don't think so,' said his father. 'Your mother means to have her way on this one. I'd best go and help her pack.'

After his dad left the room, Joe threw down his pen and let out a huge sigh. *A week at home with Nana*, he thought to himself. *Some holiday this is going to be. I bet nothing exciting happens at all.*

Joe spent the rest of the morning in his room, sulking and imagining how thoroughly boring his holiday was going to be with just him and Nana. The house was filled with the sounds of banging from the attic as his dad pulled down the suitcases and there was a medium-sized argument when his mum couldn't remember what she'd done with her passport.

'Well, what do you expect, Mike,' she shouted as she went through the drawers in the study for the third time. 'It's been so long since I've been anywhere, it's hardly surprising I can't find it.'

Eventually, the packing was finished, the passport was found and the house became calm again. Joe's dad appeared in his bedroom doorway, looking tired. 'We're just going to the shops,' he said. 'Your mum needs a few last-minute things for the holiday. We shouldn't be more than an hour ... or maybe two.'

Soon after his parents had gone out, the phone in the hallway began to ring. And, as there was only one person who ever rang them on the house phone, that meant Joe instantly knew who was calling.

He picked up the receiver. 'Hello, Nana,' he said.

'Joseph, is that you?' said a voice on the other end of the phone. 'Can you hear me? It's Nana here. Speak up, boy!'

'Yes, I know it's you, Nana,' said Joe. His

grandmother was quite hard of hearing and her telephone voice always sounded like she was trying to communicate with someone at the bottom of a very deep well. He held the phone a little further from his ear. 'How are you?'

'Who am I? I've already told you who I am, you stupid boy. It's Nana,' she snapped.

'Yes, Nana,' said Joe, wishing he could start the conversation again. 'I hear you're coming to look after me for the week.'

'I'm meant to be coming to look after you for the week,' said Nana. 'But I completely forgot that I'd agreed to go to Littlehampton with Doris Flatley to visit her sister. I'll never hear the last of it if I don't go. Tell Penny that I can't come to you after all.'

'Oh, I'm sorry to hear that,' said Joe. He was genuinely sorry because he could imagine how badly his mother was going to take this news. 'Mum and Dad are out shopping for some last-minute things,' he said. 'They were meant to be flying to Italy tonight.'

"'Well, I can't help that,' snapped Nana. 'Besides, Littlehampton is a far nicer place than Italy. There's too many flies and they eat octopus, can you imagine that?'

Joe was confused. 'They eat octopus in Littlehampton?'

'No, in Italy, you stupid boy,' said his grandmother. 'Tell Penny I'm very sorry but if I let Doris Flatley down she'll spread unpleasant gossip about me at the bridge club.'

'Shall I get Mum to call you?'

'Certainly not,' said Nana haughtily. 'I'm going to bed early and I don't want to be disturbed. Now run along and don't forget to pass on my message. Goodbye.'

The line had gone dead before Joe could answer. He replaced the receiver and rubbed his ear, which had become hot. Talking to Nana was like talking to an old lady version of his mother and just as tiring.

He really wasn't looking forward to passing on Nana's message. Either his mum would have to cancel her plans, or worse still, she might make him go with them. Either way, it was bound to make her furious and one way or another, she would find a way to blame it on him. If only he didn't have to tell them about Nana's phone call.

Then he paused. What if he didn't tell them? What if his parents just went to Italy and never got Nana's message? That wouldn't be so bad, would it?

An idea began to bloom in Joe's head and a slow smile crept across his face as he reached for his phone.

WIN!

If you've enjoyed reading about The After-School
Detective Club's adventures, read on to see
how you could WIN your very own Suffolk
adventure for your family and friends!

We're offering one lucky family a week's
break in February half-term 2023 in a luxury
4 bedroomed unique holiday home just a
stone's throw from Southwold's bustling
high street and amazing beach.

For your chance to win, simply write a
100-word review of *The Case of the Smuggler's
Curse* or *The Secret of Ragnar's Gold* – you could
tell us about your favourite scene or character.

Email your entry to:
ReviewCompetition@welbeckpublishing.com
by midnight on 30th September 2022
for your chance to win this brilliant holiday.

Competition open to residents of the UK and
Republic of Ireland only. For full T&Cs please visit:

www.welbeckpublishing.com/terms-and-conditions/review-competition

Good luck! Mark and Allan